PARSON'S HOUSE

PARSON'S HOUSE

Elizabeth Cadell

Chivers Press • Thorndike Press
Bath, England   Thorndike, Maine USA

This Large Print edition is published by Chivers Press, England, and by Thorndike Press, USA.

Published in 1999 in the U.K. by arrangement with the author's estate.

Published in 1999 in the U.S. by arrangement with Brandt & Brandt Literary Agents, Inc.

U.K. Hardcover ISBN 0–7540–3477–1 (Chivers Large Print)
U.K. Softcover ISBN 0–7540–3478–X (Camden Large Print)
U.S. Softcover ISBN 0–7862–1608–5 (General Series Edition)

The text of this Large Print edition is unabridged.
Other aspects of the book may vary from the original edition.

Set in 16 pt. New Times Roman.

Printed in Great Britain on acid-free paper.

British Library Cataloguing in Publication Data available

Library of Congress Cataloging-in-Publication Data

Cadell, Elizabeth.
        Parson's house / Elizabeth Cadell.
            p.   cm.
        ISBN 0–7862–1608–5 (lg. print : sc : alk. paper)
        1. Large type books.   I. Title.
        [PR6005.A225P37   1999]
        823'.914—dc21   98–34389

To

**Mary Paquet
of Ontario, Canada**
With love and thanks

CHAPTER ONE

The great liner, after an Atlantic crossing, docked only forty minutes behind schedule. From Montreal to Liverpool she had sailed on calm seas under cloudless skies, her decks thronged with passengers reclining on deck chairs, bounding after quoits, or splashing in the swimming pool. So warm had been the weather that after-dinner dances had been held in the open. The starlit nights had soothed old couples and stimulated young ones. Through all the ship there had been an atmosphere of enjoyment and goodwill.

But on this morning of arrival, there was no sign of goodwill and there was nothing to enjoy. The sun had vanished, giving place to mist and rain. The disembarking passengers, antlike columns bearing hand luggage, flowed into the public rooms to confront officials, stumbled up and down companionways or lined the rails to search for friends among those standing in pouring rain on the dock. Lovers, yesterday so ardent, passed one another with cold glances. Small children were located by frantic parents wandering far from the places in which they had been left. An ever-changing group milled round the purser's office to enquire for letters or telegrams. Confusion was everywhere.

1

Except on a bench on the top deck, where a young woman sat calmly, a four-year-old child on either side of her, two light-weight suitcases at her feet. She was telling the children a story, speaking English with a marked French accent.

'. . . and so you see, this mother and her two little girls—'

'What was their names?' enquired the child on her left.

'Names? The same as yours. They were called Jo, short for Joelle—and Polly, short for Jeanne-Pauline. So they—'

'Was they twins?' Joelle enquired.

'Yes. Just like you two.'

'Entickle twins,' Polly said sagely.

'That's right, identical twins. Very confusing for the general public, but no problem to their mother.' And it needn't have been a problem to their father either, she added to herself, if he'd stayed around long enough to study them and sort them out.

'Did they have a Daddy?' Polly asked.

'Yes. They—'

'Where's our Daddy?'

'He's on his way to a place called Africa, where they have something called game reserves, or maybe it's preserves; anyhow, it means that a few lucky animals will be safe inside them where your father can't get at them.'

'Why aren't we getting off this ship?' Joelle enquired.

2

'Because we don't want to be trodden underfoot. I don't know why people behave like this when a ship docks. There's no need for them to panic. Ships aren't like trains—when ships stop, they give you lots of time to get off. So we're going to sit here quietly until our friend the deck steward comes and tells us that there's a message from the purser about our car.'

'We did bring our car?' Polly asked in surprise.

'We did not. We left it at Quebec, my pet. So I've hired one to take us to Aunt Roberta's and I daresay it's down there somewhere on dry land, if you call it dry. Who would think this was mid-July?'

The question was addressed to a stewardess who had joined them, a small package in her hand.

'Normal English weather,' she explained. 'The deck steward said I'd find you here. I've brought you some chicken sandwiches, strictly under cover. You had no breakfast, Madame Brisson—I watched you. You can't drive all those miles on an empty stomach. You can eat the sandwiches now or you can eat them later, suit yourself. Jo, you'll see that your mother eats something, won't you?'

'All eat something.' Joelle had opened the package and was dividing the sandwiches with meticulous fairness.

'Good thing I multiplied by three,' the

3

stewardess commented. 'Well, I'll say goodbye. It's been nice knowing you. Look after your mother, you two, and look me up when you get back to Canada. Goodbye now.'

'Goodbye—and thanks,' Jeanne Brisson said, and as the stewardess walked away, watched her with regret. She had been well cared for during the journey. Now, for the first time, she was in sole charge of her children, their future in her hands. The prospect did not seem as stimulating as it had done during the planning stages.

As the last sandwich was eaten, the deck steward came up to announce that the hired car was waiting.

'I've put your heavy stuff into it,' he told Jeanne. 'You all set to disembark?'

'Yes.'

'Then hang on to the twins and follow me,' he instructed. 'I'll go ahead and carve a way with these two suitcases—the idea is to jab 'em into anyone who gets in the way.'

Their passage thus cleared, progress was swift except for a go-slow on the gangway to allow the children to make the most of this unusual stairway. When they reached the car, Jeanne's thanks to the steward were cut short.

'Any place, any time,' he told her. 'Enjoyed knowing you. S'long. 'Bye, kids.'

He left them and went back to the ship, which now looked to her a veritable fortress of security. She turned away from it, facing with as much courage as she could summon the unknown future.

'Now we're in France?' Jo asked.

'Not yet, Jo. We're in England. When we've stayed with Aunt Roberta for a little while, we'll go to France.'

'For always?' Polly asked.

'I daresay.'

She was taking papers from the agents. The children, as was their invariable habit when confronted with strangers, stood hand in hand, round-eyed, silent, absorbed, taking him in from head to foot. After bearing the scrutiny for a time, he paused in his paper-sorting and addressed them.

'What's the matter—something funny about me?' he asked.

There was no reply. Jo, on a downward survey of the tall figure, had reached his decorative belt. Polly, who had started at his feet, was now taking in the fancy shirt.

'They can talk—I heard them. French, are they?'

'No. I am. The twins are French-Canadians. They don't mean to be rude—they're just getting to know you.'

'*Parlez-vous français?*' he asked them.

There was no reply. Expressionless, their eyes on his face, the twins waited for more.

'No go. They don't like my accent. They've written me off,' he told Jeanne.

Adept at gauging the reactions of her

5

children, she did not contradict him. The twins climbed into the car and began to examine the interior. The agent handed Jeanne the keys and indicated a map in the pocket beside the driving wheel.

'Know your way round England?' he asked.

'No.'

'Where're you bound for?'

'Devon. A place called Rocksea—it's just a small village on the coast. I have to make for Exeter, and then I go on to a place called Hine, and after that I'll know where I am.'

'You've got a long drive. Decided on the route?'

'Yes.' She closed her eyes and recited. 'Liverpool to Chester by way of the tunnel, 18 miles. Chester to Shrewsbury, 40. Shrewsbury to Worcester, 49. Worcester to Gloucester, 27. Gloucester to Bath, 38. Bath to Taunton, 48. Taunton to Exeter, 32. Exeter to Hine roughly 14, Hine to the house I'm going to, five. Total, ship to house, 271.'

She opened her eyes to find the man's eyes fixed on her in wonder.

'What crackpot gave you that itinerary?' he asked.

'I worked it out myself.'

'With a pin?'

'It seemed a nice way to go. I wanted to see all those lovely bits of England.'

'Oh, I see.' He spoke with heavy sarcasm. 'If that's all you're after, seeing lovely bits of

6

England, that's fine. I would have said the idea would've been to get to Aunt Roberta's the quick way, before those kids wrecked the inside of the car.'

'They'll sleep a good part of the way. That's why I asked for a station wagon—room to bed them down.'

He studied the twins for a moment and then turned his eyes on their mother. He saw a small, slender figure in blue trousers and a blue-and-white striped sweater under an open waterproof jacket; a tanned face with a small nose, a wide mouth, intelligent, humorous brown eyes and an air of quiet competence. He found it difficult to sum up his impressions— nothing about her that would cause a rush of blood, he thought, and yet she had something . . .

'I suppose you wouldn't like me to sketch you out a decent, that's to say direct route?' he suggested.

She shook her head.

'No, thanks. There'll be bypasses round most of the towns, won't there?'

'I've never met a woman driver yet who took a bypass,' he told her. 'They all like crawling through the main shopping centres. Ever driven a car with these gears?'

'Some years ago, but I daresay it'll come back to me.'

'God help you if it doesn't. Well, have a good journey. The rain's stopped, anyhow.

Hope it keeps fine for you. She's a nice car—don't knock her about.'

'I won't. I hand her back at Dover, don't I?'

'That's right. Open date. You'll find all the details among those papers. So long. Nice kids, those, but I'm glad I'm not going with them on the trip.'

He opened the door and she got in and started the engine. He watched the car out of sight, shook his head, gave a shrug and walked into the pier building.

She had chosen a route, Jeanne mused as she drove towards the tunnel, but she had set no time for the journey. You couldn't make strict time-tables when you travelled in a car with children. There was no hurry. Even if they didn't arrive until midnight, Roberta would be up, and if she wasn't, the doors would be open and she would come down and—if she hadn't changed in the past ten years—would behave as casually as though wives divorced their husbands every day of the week and drove off with their children.

She felt, as she entered the tunnel, that she was driving from a dark past towards a happier future. Whatever lay ahead, she thought, must be better than the two years of her father's last illness, and the five years she had spent trying to make her marriage work. Roberta's telegram had offered an interval during which she could rest, relax, make plans for herself and her children. She would be in a familiar setting, among old friends; everything would work itself out.

'Where's Aunt Roberta?' Jo asked after a time.

'A long, long way away. We have to drive a long time before we get there. You've got books to look at, and sultanas to chew if you feel funny, and apples and pears, and you can play that new game with Polly and when you feel sleepy, you can curl up under the rug and have a nice nap. We'll stop a lot—for a nice sandwich lunch, and for tea, and even perhaps for supper if there's a lot of traffic on the roads and we get held up. And tomorrow morning, when you wake up, there'll be a beach to play on, and rocks and pools and it'll be lovely.'

Lovely . . . It had been lovely—ten years ago. What had given those holidays at Rocksea their special flavour, she wondered? What had there been, after all? A white house built on a promontory overlooking, in summer, a blue bay, at other seasons a white froth of surf. A cottage next door. Below, a small, sandy beach flanked by rocks and cut off at high tide from the neighbouring beaches, so that they could call it, virtually, their own. Five children; you couldn't count the sixth, Oliver Hobart, because he belonged to the house. Five children, all about the same age, at school in England, their relations for various reasons unable or unwilling to receive them for holidays. She and Paul Brisson had been the only foreigners; the others were English: Austin Parkes, only son of a millionaire who had once owned large estates in Jamaica; Elva Royce, whose parents divided their time between their house in London and their house in the Bahamas—and Roberta Murray, whose parents lived in Italy, but not together. Jeanne had been ten when she first went to stay with the man and woman they called Uncle David and Aunt Lorna. She had been fifteen when her mother died and her father left France and went to Canada, taking her with him. Paul Brisson had been the next to leave; he, too, went to Canada but Jeanne had not met him again until she was nineteen.

She had harboured no regrets at leaving her English school, but she had missed bitterly the holidays at Rocksea. The exchange of letters, briskly begun, had through the years become intermittent but had never entirely ceased.

It was Roberta who had sent the telegram.

Elva and I renting Oliver's cottage suggest you share.

Before the letter which followed it reached her, Jeanne had cabled an acceptance. The doubts and hesitations that had filled her mind since her divorce vanished; the struggle to decide what would be best for the children ceased. The thought of finding a temporary home, a halting-place between past and future; above all, the chance to talk freely to people of her own age and outlook, proved irresistible.

She had not thought of going to England; what was there for her but childish memories? But the telegram had made it seem the obvious place to go.

The letter, when it came, had given few details, but from what it said and did not say Jeanne was able to form an idea of how the plan would work. Roberta explained that she found London too distracting; she had work to do and wanted to do it in peace. Elva had come to the end of a period of historical research and wanted a quiet retreat in which to assemble her notes. They would both be busy, Roberta said, and Jeanne would be free to spend her days on the beach with the children. There had been no mention of cooking or housework, but neither Roberta nor Elva, Jeanne remembered, had been of the type to interest themselves in domestic details. If running the house was to be left to her, she would be content, for not since she had kept house for her father had she known what it was to have control of a household. Her husband's great-aunts had run the Quebec house and they had also—during her frequent absences with Paul—looked after the twins. Now, while Roberta and Elva were busy, she could be busy too.

She halted for lunch at a roadside hotel which had a small garden at the back. Tables on the lawn, budgerigars in a large aviary to keep the children interested, milk and cold

11

chicken and salad, vanilla ices for the twins, coffee for herself, a wash-and-brush-up in a white-tiled bathroom and then back to the car for more mileage. Supper inside a comfortable roadhouse, with rain beginning to fall again. Then a long drive through the wet, dark Devon countryside with two sleeping children in the back of the car.

Exeter. Another fourteen miles and they'd be in Hine, and then two miles and the turning to the left, and left again for Rocksea.

She had told the car-hire agent that she would know where she was when she reached Hine, but when she was a mile or so out of the town, she realised that she was lost. She had no idea how she had missed her way—she had taken the turn to the left and at first she had recognised landmarks—two churches, a steep rise and a gradual descent. After that there should have been a turning leading into quiet lanes, but the side road had led to another main road, and there were no signs with place-names that she recognised.

She saw a group of buildings ahead, and decided to stop and ask the way. She drew up at a small, well-lighted hotel, entered the reception hall and addressed the sleepy-looking old man seated behind the desk.

'Good evening. Could you tell me how I can get to a village named Rocksea? It can't be far away—it's not far from Hine. I thought I knew where I was, but it's some time since I was here.'

'That's for sure,' he said. 'You won't call Rocksea a village when you get to it. It was eight years ago they built the Corby bypass through it. Sliced it in two. Since then, it's been mushrooming. Soon be a good-sized town. Which half d'you want? Are you making for the sea half, or the inland half?'

'The house I'm going to overlooks the sea.'

'Then you shouldn't be on this road. Go back to the crossroads, turn right a couple of miles farther on, right again at the Cromwell Arms and then keep going.'

'Thank you.'

He came round the desk and accompanied her to the door.

'I used to know the old village once,' he said. 'There weren't many houses then. I had a niece used to work at one of the houses on the promontory—Parson's House, they called it. Know it?'

She did not tell him how well she had known it. She said merely that she was on her way to the cottage next door to it.

'Ah, that was the one the parson moved to,' he said. 'But it was the big one, the one he built, they called Parson's House. Nobody's ever called it anything else, nor ever will. In these parts, once a name sticks, it goes on sticking. It's a dirty night. Can I get you a cup of tea or coffee before you go?'

'No, thank you. I've left my children in the

13

car.'

'Children?' She was accustomed to the note of surprise; strangers invariably subtracted several years from her age. 'You got children?'

'Yes. Two.'

'How old?'

'Twins of four. I'd like to see them home and dry.'

'Home, maybe. Dry, no. We've had rain all through the summer and there's no sign of anything better on the way. Good night. Good luck.'

The children had not wakened. She drove on through the darkness, recalling the little village of Rocksea as she had known it and trying to imagine it grown into a town and sliced in half. The new road, she thought, must have been taken between the promontory and the wide, windswept heath known as Rockcommon. If so, it wouldn't be far from Parson's House and the four neighbouring houses. It would be strange to hear heavy traffic in a place in which she remembered chiefly carts and bicycles. And here it was, the new road, but for the next three miles the rain was coming down too steadily to allow her to see more than a few yards ahead. There ought to be a turning . . . yes, this was it, narrow and stony as it had been the last time she had clattered along it in Uncle David's pony trap.

As the car approached the sea, the rain ceased. The noise of the traffic fell away, and

14

by the time she turned on to the road that ran behind the five houses overlooking the sea, it was no more than a drone. She could see the outline of the buildings; the largest of them, Parson's House, looked dark and shuttered, which seemed unnatural in July. But Uncle David was dead and so was Aunt Lorna, and she felt she would rather see the house empty than filled with strangers.

After driving another hundred yards, she came to the low, wooden, well-remembered gate of the cottage next door. It was wide open, and with a sudden access of happiness, she told herself that its arms were open in welcome.

She drove round the side of the cottage and stopped at the kitchen door. The clock in the car told her that it was close on midnight, but the door, like the gate, was wide open. In the light streaming from the kitchen she could see a tall figure in trousers and a loose sweater. Roberta? Not possible. Roberta had been short and fat, with very fair, very wiry hair, and a plain, flat face. This girl—woman—was slim, with a glistening satin curtain of hair falling smoothly to her shoulders. Her features were an attractive blend of slightly upturned nose, large mouth and narrow, long-lashed eyes. Then she spoke, and Jeanne heard an unchanged Roberta whose speech ran on and on, a careless outpouring without pause and without the smallest interest in any effect her

15

frank opinions might have on listeners.

'Hello, Jeanne. Welcome back. I worked out how long you'd take, but it was no use because I didn't know what time you'd start. I rang the shipping office in Exeter, but they were all complete idiots and not one of them could tell me a thing about your time of arrival. Let me look at you.'

She waited for Jeanne to get out of the car, and studied her.

'Totally unchanged,' she said. 'Which I didn't expect. I thought you'd look old and ravaged, I don't know why, maybe because I felt that marrying and having children and divorcing your husband must be aging processes. How was the trip?'

'Fine. I feel old, but not ravaged. How's everything, Roberta?'

'Not bad—but I haven't fitted quite as much into the last ten years as you have. Let's take a look at those twins.' She peered into the car. 'Two of a kind. But not like you, and not like Paul, so who?'

'My mother.'

'What do we do now—wake them up?'

'They won't wake—at least, not fully. Can you carry one of them?'

'I can carry both of them. Have you forgotten that I could lift you over my head? I could still do it—you're still pocket size.'

'Before we take the twins in, I'd like to say thank you. Your telegram was a life-saver.'

16

'Why? Hadn't you made up your mind what you were going to do?'

'More or less. I was going to France, to my father's relations. But I hardly remember them, and I wasn't ready to ... well, thank you.'

'You're welcome. That's twice I've said it. Elva and I happened to be talking about the divorce, and suddenly we thought it would be nice if you could share the cottage.'

'Is she here?'

'No. She's supposed to be coming in a few days, but she's not what you could call predictable. Incidentally, the cottage isn't the same as it used to be. Come inside and look.'

Jeanne went in, looked round the room and gave an exclamation of surprise.

'*Tiens!*'

'As you say. Like it?'

'It's ... it's lovely!'

The kitchen, as she remembered it, had been a very long, shabby room with a door at the end leading to a sunless sitting room. The wall between the two rooms was now a wide arch, one side of which was a kitchen with modern fitments; the other side was a sitting room with two small tables and comfortable chairs. Dividing the two sections was an oval dining table. The small, diamond-paned windows had been replaced by wide ones giving an uninterrupted view of the sea.

Roberta was opening a door.

'Here's what used to be the hall,' she said. 'Now only half of it's a hall. The other half's a bathroom.'

'Is upstairs different too?'

'No. Same as before. Elva and I are in the two attic rooms, and Oliver's in his own room, the one over the kitchen. He wouldn't rent us the cottage until we'd agreed to let him use it for occasional weekends. I've put you and the twins into the downstairs bedroom because you can go straight out to the garden, if you can call it a garden. You can use the downstairs bathroom; we'll use the one upstairs.'

'When was all this done?' Jeanne asked as they walked back to the car.

'Lorna had it done at intervals, when she'd saved enough money. She started improving it when she and David realised they'd never own Parson's House—that's to say, David would never own it, so he would never be able to leave it to her. I've made my room into a kind of studio. I'm going to paint.'

Jeanne spoke in surprise.

'Paint? You mean write, don't you?'

'No, I don't mean write. I mean paint.'

'But you—'

'Yes, I know. That damned crab. Did he travel as far as Canada?'

'Of course. Every child I know there had a Sideways book.'

'Every child here, too,' Roberta said morosely. 'I'm sick to death of Sideways. If it

18

hadn't been for Austin Parkes, there would never have been a book about Sideways at all. Pure interference, but then Austin's—'

'You mean you didn't want—'

'—to put him into a book? Of course I didn't. I simply used to draw him and tell stories about him to amuse children, when I met any children. Then Austin took some of the drawings to this man he knew who knew a man who knew a publisher, and now Sideways, who used to be fun, is famous and everybody thinks I'm going to draw more of him.'

'And you're not?'

'Never. Never, never. My God, do you think I want to spend the rest of my life writing about crabs? I'm going to paint. I'm painting tiles, working on my own designs. The designs . . . but you'll see tomorrow. Come and get the twins out.'

Jeanne opened the car door.

'I'll take the near one,' Roberta said. 'Which one is it?'

'Joelle.'

'Can anyone tell them apart?'

'Not at first. Can I heat some milk for them?'

'Do just whatever you like. For them or for yourself. You're paying a third of the rent, so you're entitled to make yourself at home.'

They carried the children into a bedroom that had once been Paul Brisson's. In addition to the single bed, there were now two cots.

'I hired the cots,' Roberta said, lowering Jo into one of them. 'There's not much room, but you won't be spending much time indoors. This weather has to change—we've been drowned all through July, so in spite of what the weather reports say, I think we'll get some sun soon. Look at me—I've hardly started to tan. Last year at this time I looked like a beautiful bronze statue. Well, a bronze statue, but really sensational.'

They undressed the children. Jeanne took milk from the refrigerator, warmed it, and they drank slowly and sleepily. Then they were tucked in and Jeanne put out the light and followed Roberta to the kitchen.

'How about you?' Roberta asked. 'Hungry?'

'Yes.'

'There's bread and cheese, and things in cans, help yourself. I didn't know anything about children's diets, so I left it to you. Tomorrow morning you can go shopping. We've got real shops here now—not just those little ones in the front rooms of the cottages. Did you see much of Rocksea as you drove through?'

'No. Not enough visibility. I hear it's almost a town.'

'You'll see. It was beginning to grow even before they made the through road. When they built it, these five houses on the promontory got cut off from the rest. They took away the cottages and took the new road along the edge

20

of Rockcommon and we got left—marooned—on this side. The other side of the road is nearly all new: church, pub, school, shops, houses, not to mention a four-star hotel.'

'What happened to the people in the cottages?'

'They were given some kind of compensation—not enough, they said—and moved to houses in the new part. If you're looking for the cheese, it's in that cup-board.'

Jeanne placed bread, butter and cheese on the table.

'Who lives in the other houses along here?' she asked.

'Parson's House is empty. Old Mrs Datchet—remember her?—is still at Ranchers, but her son and her daughter live with her now. You'll see them when they come back from Scotland—they spend a month there every year.'

'And Boris?'

Roberta laughed.

'I didn't think you'd be able to forget Boris. She still lives at Vistamar. At the moment she's in London.'

'Is Trotter still with her?'

'Yes. And the dogs. Not the dogs you knew when you were here, but still Great Danes. Does that cover all the neighbours?'

'Not all. Who's living at Boulders? Is old Mr Hollis still alive?'

21

'No. He died about four years ago. He got crazier and crazier.'

'Who's in the house?'

Roberta lit a cigarette.

'Ugandans,' she answered. 'Or more accurately, Indians. Do you remember that Uganda-for-the-Ugandans upheaval some years ago when—'

'I remember. All those Indians who had British passports.'

'That's right. Well, you know that Mr Hollis had spent most of his life in Uganda, in business, and he'd kept in touch with his old employees. So when they got turned out, he sent for his ex-chief clerk and offered him rooms in the house. The clerk came, and he brought his grandson, and the grandson brought his wife—all of sixteen years old, she was—and she brought her mother and they all settled down at Boulders.'

'How did Rocksea like that?'

'Everybody rallied—led by Boris and Lorna and David. David got jobs in Hine for Grandfather and the grandson. The wife and her mother stayed at home and looked after Mr Hollis. When he died, he left the house to Grandfather, and some money to go with it.'

'And they're still there?'

'Yes. Mother runs the house. The other three—Grandfather, grandson and wife— opened a little shop in Rocksea. It's called the Spice Box.'

'They own it?'

'Yes. Mr Hollis's inheritance. It's doing well—I'll take you there tomorrow. They don't sell anything but—as you might guess—spices, but they've made Rocksea curry-conscious. That brings you up to date with all the houses along the promontory. What else do you want to know?'

'What's Elva's job?'

'Historical research is what she calls it. At the moment, she's working for a professor who's writing a book on the Crusades. I'm going to make coffee—want some?'

'Please.'

Roberta left her chair and went in an abstracted way from cupboard to cupboard assembling coffee, coffee pot, cups and saucers. These she placed in front of Jeanne, and resumed her seat.

'I don't know what you're going to make of Elva,' she said. 'She's a bit of a mess, one way and another—I mean her appearance. She could be attractive, if she gave her mind to it, but the trouble is, she doesn't care what she looks like. If she'd listen to me, she could be a knockout.' She paused. Jeanne, remembering stringy hair, thick round glasses and uneven teeth, was looking surprised. 'I know you find it hard to believe, but you'll see. Her figure's nice and her teeth got straightened out and her glasses suit her and if she took care of her hair, it could look quite decent. But her clothes are terrible, honestly terrible. Austin told her she looked like an actress dressed for the part of a Lithuanian peasant, and he was right, but then again, he was wrong because she's not the peasant type. She's got something, I wouldn't like to call it dignity, but it's a sort of calm poise. You only have to look at her to see she's brainy. I used to hope her mother would do something to smarten her up, but she never came near her, and now she's dead. She died over a year ago, and since then, Elva's made the excuse that she can't afford to spend money on clothes. Or money on anything.'

'I thought her father had a lot of money.'

'He has. But since her mother died, Elva hasn't seen much of it. In fact, for a time she didn't see any. She met her father at her mother's funeral, and after that, for all he knew, Elva could have been dead and buried too. She didn't worry—she'd never thought of him as a parent anyway. Then about a year ago the bank manager in Hine—of all people—made her father fix a sort of settlement on her—not much, but added to what she earns, it could pay for a decent wardrobe, if she was interested.'

'Doesn't she ever see him?'

'See her father? Never. She knows he's still living in his house in London, but she hasn't been inside it since her mother died. I don't know why I worry about her, but every time I see her, I want to get her to a hairdresser and drag her to a boutique. Some men like her, don't ask me why—and don't ask her either, because she doesn't seem to know they're there. One of them got really interested, but he said it was horse work, and gave up. Then there was one who got as far as buying tickets and getting her to the Rome plane in time, but I never found out whether he got anything for his trouble. I've come to the conclusion that she's sexless. She . . . Wait a minute; I've just remembered there was a picture of her in a newspaper a couple of weeks ago. I kept it—I think.' She searched through several drawers, decided she must have thrown it away, walked to the other side of the archway and returned with the paper in her hand. 'Got it.' She showed Jeanne a small picture of a group taken outside a large building, and pointed. 'There's Elva. It's small, but it's clear. Would you have recognised her?'

'Yes, easily.' Jeanne was reading the caption. 'But it says they were all going to South America for four months.'

'They weren't. Not all of them. Elva and the professor were just seeing the others off. But don't you see, that's *typical*—the reporter simply didn't *register*. If she hadn't looked so dreary, he wouldn't have lumped her with all the others, and left it at that.'

Jeanne handed back the newspaper.

'What's Austin doing?' she asked.

'Austin? He's busy giving away all the riches his father and grandfather piled up.'

25

Jeanne paused in the act of biting into a cheese sandwich.

'*Giving?*'

'That's right. Handing it out. He always had a guilty feeling about his money, don't you remember? He said it all came from exploitation, and you looked it up in the dictionary and found it meant grinding the faces of the poor natives, wherever. He inherited it when he was twenty-five—not only money; land, houses, shares, companies, you name it, he owns it. And then he began to hand it out.'

'*All* of it?'

'All the part that came from grinding faces. He's a one-man charitable foundation. No office, no staff, no overheads—except Oliver, who does his accounts. Could you do that— give away all your riches if you had any?'

'I don't know.'

Roberta refilled her cup and lit another cigarette.

'Do you notice that I haven't said one single word about Paul? I mean, about you and Paul?' she asked.

'Yes. What do you want to know?'

'Everything. But not tonight. I'm saving it for the morning. I'll only make one comment: we all knew it wouldn't last. When we heard you'd married him, we all sat back and waited for the break-up.'

'Why?'

'Because you didn't go together, he and you. Austin said he was sure you wouldn't have fallen in love if the two of you hadn't met again in Canada and remembered the old days and reminisced yourselves into a sentimental mood.'

'We—'

'No. Tomorrow, with all the intimate details. You won't keep anything back?'

'Nothing. Have you given up your studio in London?'

'Yes. I don't think I'll go back there. I'm getting old or something—I used to like the London racket, but I don't any more. When I'm working at anything, I like to be quiet, and in London you can't keep people away. They drop in, you get out the drinks, and the next thing, they've settled down for a week. And parties tend to be the same ones over and over again in different places, and if you do happen to meet someone you like the look of, you can't get through to him because there's too much screeching going on.'

'Does Oliver work in London?'

'Only sometimes. He gave up his accountant's job and now he's on his own, sometimes in London but more often in Exeter.'

'When exactly did Uncle David die?'

'Fifteenth of April, but what I didn't tell you in my letter was that no sooner was he buried than Lorna got a letter from Maurice Selby asking—no, not asking, telling her to get out.'

'Get out?'

'Get out of Parson's House. He owns it.'

'Who does?'

'I've just told you. Maurice Selby. David's brother.'

'I didn't know David had a brother.'

'None of us knew as children, because he was never mentioned. He and David had a terrible row when David married Lorna. He refused to sell the house to David—Oliver said it was because he hated Lorna. He thought Lorna had come between him and his brother. In the end, he agreed to rent the house and the furniture to David, but as soon as he was dead, he turned Lorna out.'

'Where did Lorna go?'

'She came back here. She only brought her personal belongings, nothing else. Some of the furniture at Parson's House was hers, but she left it there. She never got over being turned out—it really was a ghastly thing to do to her, so soon after David died. She didn't seem well, and Oliver thought a sea trip might do her good, so she picked a cruise and went at the end of May. She left instructions that if she died before she got home, she was to be buried at sea. She did, and she was—somewhere in the English Channel, right in sight of home.'

'What's going to happen to Parson's House?'

'Brother Maurice is going to live in it, as he

28

did before David married Lorna.'

'Is he going to live there alone?'

'No. He married a year or so ago. His wife runs a sort of picture gallery, but she must have given it up, because they've sold their house in London and they're coming to live here. The house is being done up—you'll see the scaffolding in the morning. I hope there's a nice big tidal wave just as they get settled.'

'A tidal wave would—'

'I know. Wash us away too. Somehow, I can't imagine Parson's House without Lorna.'

'Did you come down here much, after we all left?'

'Whenever I could. Elva was here most of the time. Austin came and went, but he always stayed in this cottage with Oliver. Lorna never seemed to change. Why did we all love her so much when we were young?'

'She was kind. And she was beautiful. And she made a home for us.'

'They were wonderful times, weren't they? It was probably just like anywhere else, but we didn't think so. What do you remember chiefly?'

'Lorna, always waiting for me at the door when David brought me from Exeter station. We never had to knock—she was always there, waiting. What do you remember?'

'Food. Oh, that lovely food, after the bilge and the sludge of school meals! Hot toast and homemade jam for breakfast, and great

29

pitchers of milk, and hot scones for tea, with jam and Devonshire cream, and steaming soups or stews in winter, and fish we'd caught ourselves, and lovely slushy milk puddings, and hot chocolate last thing at night, and David going miles to try and find those old-time ginger-beer stone jars, because we loved taking them on picnics.' She got up, walked to the door and stood looking out into the darkness. 'When I come out here at night,' she told Jeanne over her shoulder, 'and when I look up at Parson's House, I always think I can see Lorna. Remember how she and David used to sit on that terrace on fine nights, listening to the sea?'

'Yes.'

'Well, I don't see him, but I see a sort of white blur, like those floating dresses Lorna used to wear in summer.'

Jeanne came to stand beside her.

'Does Oliver talk much about her?' she asked.

'No. If the subject comes up, he doesn't change it, but he doesn't say much. He misses her. They were always pretty close.' Her tone became reminiscent. 'We were a pretty unsettled lot when we first came here. There was you with not a soul you knew in England— apart from school—and not able to go home because your mother was so ill, and there was me with my parents separated, and Elva with parents who as far as anyone could see had

30

forgotten all about her, and Austin with a
father all over the place but never where he
wanted him. I remember when I came to
Parson's House the first time, I told myself I'd
behave so badly and create such hell that my
parents would have to do something about it.
But that wasn't how it worked out. I didn't
expect it would be ... well, the way it was.
Maybe it was the house, maybe it was David
and Lorna, but whatever it was, it was
wonderful. I didn't expect a lovely room of my
own, and nothing said about rules or keeping
to our own part of the house or not being
allowed to do this or that. It was like coming to
a real home, and then there was all that
bicycling to the farms and riding the farmers'
horses all over Rockcommon. You won't see
many fields now, and there aren't any paths to
ride along or bike along. No more—' She
broke off abruptly. 'Jeanne, can you see that?'

Jeanne, following her glance, looked up at
the dark outline of Parson's House.

'See what?' she asked.

'Up there. Near the bench. Something
white.'

'I can see a sort of gleam on the bench.
That's because the bench is wet and the—'

'Can't you see a white blur?'

'No.'

'Sure?'

'Quite sure.'

'Then I must be smoking too much.' She

31

followed Jeanne into the kitchen and closed the door behind them. 'Let's go to bed. We've got a lot of talking to do in the morning.'

They put the cups into the dish-washing machine and turned out the light. Roberta paused on her way upstairs.

'Not that I'd mind seeing Lorna,' she told Jeanne. 'She'd make an elegant ghost.'

Jeanne, at the door of her ground floor bedroom, stared up at her.

'You believe in ghosts?' she asked in surprise.

'I do and I don't. I had one of my own in London. He used to come through the studio skylight on foggy nights and climb into my bed.'

'Did you get out and sleep on the sofa?'

'No sofa. He kept to his side, I kept to mine. In the morning, there was only me. Sometimes I wonder what he'll do when winter comes and he finds I'm not there.'

'You don't think he'll follow you down here, do you?'

'He might. What'll you do if he does?'

'Nothing. I'll just remove myself and the twins, that's all. Good night.'

CHAPTER TWO

Parson's House, built in the early nineteen-twenties, was the first building to be erected on

32

some neglected acres of land that thrust out towards the sea from the little hamlet of Rocksea. This promontory had been considered too exposed, too wild and rocky for residential purposes, and Rocksea had remained a cluster of cottages cowering between the rocks and the wide inland expanse known as Rockcommon. The nearest town was Hine, five miles away.

To Hine had come the parson, newly appointed to the living. After inspecting the parsonage—a rambling, decrepit building his predecessors had uncomplainingly occupied—he stated flatly that it would not do for him. The ensuing dispute involved the Bishop, several of the neighbouring clergy and both urban and rural authorities, and ended only when the parson was permitted to build his own house at his own expense on a site of his own choice.

A sea-lover, he searched for a sea view and came upon Rocksea. Between the rocks on the promontory he discovered scrub-covered expanses, and on the largest and highest of these built a commodious, graceful house which he named Thassala. The building did not fit into any recognisable architectural style or period, but the parson was content, having succeeded in incorporating into the structure all his dreams: balconies with delicate wrought-iron railings, Dutch gables, French windows, Greek pillars and a maximum of light and air. With so much to please him, he was prepared to put up with the lack of local amenities.

This lack was soon supplied, for where the parson had led, speculative builders followed. To one side of, and on a lower level than the parson's house rose a cottage which, like the parson's house, was the embodiment of the builder's dreams. It combined strong construction with fancy trimmings, like a stout tree bearing delicate new leaves. Planned as a small dwelling, it had at first three rooms downstairs and, above them, two attics with small, circular windows that looked like a pair of giant binoculars trained on to the sea. Then the builder, carried away, added a very long kitchen and over it built another bedroom. He named the cottage Lowcot, and successive owners were to strive in vain to grow trees round it in order to give it its natural woodland setting.

Next to spring up, on the other side of the parson's house, was a villa modelled on Spanish lines, its chief feature an enclosed patio which performed the dual function of providing shelter from the strong sea breezes and excluding all but the midday sun. Next appeared Ranchers, brain-child of a builder who read Westerns—a low, flat-roofed, white-painted house which squatted in the surrounding scrub and gave a Mexican touch to the scene.

Adjoining Vistamar, the pseudo-Spanish villa, was the last available site. Being the rockiest, it remained for some time unsold. It was eventually bought by a couple who, unable to meet the cost of getting rid of the rocks, built a house round them. The result was interesting, but not comfortable. It was called, appropriately, Boulders, and like Lowcot, Vistamar and Ranchers, was known by its correct name. But the parson's house remained Parson's House.

The parson's only child, a daughter named Lorna, was born in the house. When she was in her early teens, rising prices, his imminent retirement and the threat of a second world war forced the parson to sell his beloved home. Reluctant to leave the view he had grown to love so much, he used the proceeds of the sale to buy the cottage next door, and moved into it with his wife and child. Here he, and later his wife, died, and here, years later, returned his widowed daughter Lorna Hobart and her small son Oliver.

Lorna took some time to settle down. The cottage, empty throughout the war, had since had a series of tenants. It needed repair and redecoration, but she had little beyond her widow's pension and could undertake no improvements. She sometimes looked with a touch of envy at the house her father had built. As a child, she had left it without regret, eager to move to the cottage next door with its inglenooks and tiny windows with diamond panes, unable to understand her parents' preference for the house they were leaving. Now she could better understand how they had felt.

The house was occupied by two brothers, sons of the rich manufacturer named Selby who had bought it from the parson. Both brothers worked in the family firm which had its main office in London and a branch in Exeter. Maurice, the elder, was a cold, unfriendly man who had as little as possible to do with his neighbours. David, younger by some years, was sensitive, quiet and kindly, and came to be more and more interested in the pretty widow next door. If she was aware of his growing admiration, she gave no sign.

David knew that his brother disliked her, but he was totally unprepared for the storm which broke when he announced his intention of marrying her. The situation was awkward, for both house and furniture belonged to Maurice, and he refused to consider David's offer of buying them. He believed that the widow was marrying solely in order to get back into the house her father had built, and was convinced that the marriage would not last. He decided after a time to rent the house and the furniture to David, while he himself moved to London.

When Lorna moved to the big house after the wedding, there was no question of selling

36

the cottage. David's income came from a trust fund which would revert to the firm; in the event of his death, there would be little he could leave his widow.

Any hope of a reconciliation with Maurice ended when Lorna persuaded David to allow her to take in during school holidays children whose parents were abroad. She liked children, and remembered an unhappy period during her own schooldays when she had had no home to go to. Five children had come—three girls who were accommodated at Parson's House, and two boys who shared the cottage with Oliver. So successfully had the first holiday passed that the five visitors returned again and again, resisting all attempts on the part of their parents or guardians to persuade them to go somewhere else for a change.

It was five years before the arrangement came to an end. Two of the children—Jeanne and Paul—left England for Canada. The other three continued to come, at first regularly, later intermittently, but they had never lost touch with Lorna Selby, or with one another.

Now, with one exception, they were to be together again. But not at Parson's House.

*   *   *

On the morning following Jeanne's arrival, the weather seemed to be making amends—the

37

sun shone, the sea sparkled. Coming down to the kitchen, Roberta stood surveying the scene: the twins, raised on cushions to table-height, were eating their cereal. Opposite sat Jeanne, buttering toast.

'I'll paint you all as you are,' she remarked, 'and call it Round The Trough.'

Jeanne thought that it was Roberta who would have been a painter's choice. Her clothes, like those she had worn the night before, were simple, but of expensive material and superb cut. She put her thoughts into words.

'With a figure like yours,' she said, 'I suppose you look nice in anything.'

'With a figure like mine, I look best in nothing. Any spare coffee?'

'Yes. Lots.'

'What are those children staring at?'

'They're just—'

'—classifying me? What language do I have to address them in?'

'French or English, preferably English. Toast?'

'No, nothing to eat. Just black coffee.'

'Are you coming shopping with us, or are you going to stay home and work?'

'I'm not in a working mood. I was thinking about your car in the night—can't you return it to the hire firm? How long did you arrange to keep it?'

'Open date. I didn't know how long you'd let

38

us stay.'

'You can stay as long as you want to. It's crazy to rush off to relations in France that you haven't seen for years and years. Where's nicer in summer than here? The weather's changed—look, sunshine. And a beach practically to ourselves. Why not settle down until you've got your future properly sorted out?'

'I'd like to.'

'Then get rid of your car and use mine. It's small and it's old, but it goes all right once you get it started. If I spent less on clothes, I could spend more on cars. Elva won't buy a car—she thinks people ought to use public transport. She's got a lot of peculiar ideas of that kind. It's a pity you've got to go shopping on a lovely morning like this, but it was no use my getting in a lot of stores you didn't want.'

'I've made a list. We needn't take long.'

'There's a supermarket,' Roberta told the twins, 'and outside it there's a little playground with swings and slides, so you can enjoy yourselves while your mother and I do the shopping.—Unnerving, those stares,' she complained to Jeanne. 'Do they ever utter?'

'All the time, once they've got you labelled.'

They went out soon after breakfast in Jeanne's car. When they reached the last house on the promontory and turned inland, Jeanne saw for the first time the changes that had taken place in Rocksea. She stopped the car and sat gazing in wonder.

'Heavens!' she said.

'I thought you were going to say *Tiens* again. It doesn't look as it used to, does it?'

Jeanne shook her head slowly. The cottages had vanished. So had the duckpond, the fields and most of Rockcommon. In their place was a wide highway, and beyond it a town—small, neat, well-planned, with a central square lined with flower beds and benches. Behind the square was a shopping complex. A tree-bordered road circled the town on the far side, smaller streets radiating from it and leading to a new residential district.

'Like it?' Roberta asked at last.

'Yes. Well, in a way, yes.'

'That's how everybody reacts. They start off liking it and then reaction sets in and they begin to make speeches about what a pity it looks so new and doesn't fit into the traditional Devon pattern. Oliver says there was a split right down the middle when it came to planning. One half wanted an overgrown village with picturesque cottages. The other half wanted this, and got it. There's great competition to come and live here—people from Hine want to come, and people from Exeter want to buy land for weekend cottages, but can't find any.'

'Why not? There's still a lot of un-built-on land.'

'There's also a strict unofficial immigration

40

quota. No trouble about colour or religion; you can be brown or black or white and you can pray on a prayer mat or with a prayer wheel or against a wailing wall and nobody minds. But if you want to come here, you can't put up sky-scrapers or multi-level biscuit-box apartments. You have to submit plans and do what you're told. Not like the good old days, Oliver says, when his grandfather and those other four pioneers got on to the promontory and built what they fancied. See the sign on that hotel, and on the pub next to it?'

Jeanne looked at them:

CRISTALL'S HOTEL & RESTAURANT

and the humbler building adjoining it:

THE LION INN

'Both signs designed and painted by me,' Roberta said. 'I asked Mr Cristall if I could do them, and he let me. He even paid me. I had a bit of trouble with the lion's head, but it came all right in the end. Remember Mr Cristall?'

'No.'

'Well, I suppose not; he only came back to Rocksea about six years ago. The town's terribly proud of him.'

Rocksea had reason to be proud: Mr Cristall was the first and so far the only one of its sons to make the rags-to riches ascent. He

41

had started life in one of the little cottages which Jeanne remembered and which had been demolished to make room for the new road. The son of a shepherd, one of nine children, he had gone to work at the age of fourteen in a small and struggling pub in Hine called the Hopscotch. Sturdy, cheerful, hard-working, he had so impressed the publican that on his death the young Cristall, aged twenty, found himself the heir and possessor of the business.

He did not keep it; he sold it and went to France and Italy for a long training in hotel management. Returning to England, he joined the staff of a modest hotel in Soho. At the age of forty, he bought it and turned ten of its thirty rooms into a restaurant. Within a short space of time, it might have been possible to book a room at Cristall's Hotel, but there was never an empty seat in the restaurant.

It was Austin Parkes who, on Oliver's suggestion, invited Mr Cristall to build the first hotel in Rocksea. He provided the land and half the money, and the project included not only Cristall's hotel but also the adjacent pub, the Lion. Mr Cristall contributed the other half of the money and his outgoing, genial, sociable personality, which had done so much to make his London venture a success. Having installed his brothers and sisters in key positions in all the establishments, he divided his time between Soho and Rocksea, keeping a room for himself in both hotels, but spending most of his leisure at the Lion, sometimes offering, sometimes accepting a drink, making or renewing acquaintance with the customers. He knew everybody and everything in Rocksea and Hine, was an inveterate gossip and a firm friend of both Oliver and Austin.

'When he told people he was going to build a good hotel here, they thought he was crazy,' Roberta said. 'But look at it: not too many rooms, only two storeys high, comfortable, and with perfect food. The restaurant's famous— even people from abroad have heard of it— what are you laughing at?'

'You. You sound—'

'—as though I'm trying to sell the place? Well, I feel that way. I didn't see it until it was looking more or less as you see it now—I was travelling round, shuttling between my mother and my father. When I came down to see David and Lorna, I had a sort of pang thinking of the duckpond, but then I felt a wave of pride. My town. Why not? I've never had roots anywhere else, so why shouldn't I adopt Rocksea? It's still growing, but more slowly. And we can't sit here and watch it grow— we've got shopping to do. Let's go.'

They went on, entered the wide road and left it shortly afterwards to drive along a street lined with shops. Arriving at the supermarket, they left the children in the miniature park in which twenty or more children were playing,

43

watched over by an elderly woman who sat knitting on a bench until it was necessary for her to rise and admonish the unruly or pick up and comfort the fallen.

'Got the list?' Roberta asked as she and Jeanne went into the building.

'Yes.'

'You'll find things expensive. I hope you got a lot of alimony out of Paul.'

'He provided very generously for the children. I didn't want anything. I've got a little money of my own. I didn't want to take his.'

'Why not?'

'Because I thought that if you give up a job—which I did—you can't expect to go on being paid.'

'I suppose that's one way of looking at it. You were going to be a nurse, weren't you?'

'No. A teacher. I couldn't go on training for anything because when my father got ill, I had to look after him. Then he died, and I got married, and then there were the twins and . . . well, here I am.'

'Any idea what you'd like to work at?'

'Only one—rather vague. I have an aunt in Tours who has a nursery school. She's sixty, and I thought she might let me join her and perhaps take over in time. That would solve the problem of what to do with the twins until they're older. I don't want to take a job and leave them with someone else—not while they're small.'

44

'Have they taken in the fact that they're not going to see their male parent any more?'

'Paul can see them any time he wants to. If you mean do they miss him . . . No. There's nothing to miss. He was never there. They'll miss his aunts, and the aunts will miss them—terribly.'

Shopping did not take long. They put their purchases into the car and walked to the playground to fetch the twins, but when they got there, Roberta led Jeanne to an empty bench.

'The twins are quite happy,' she said. 'So we can talk. I want to hear about you and Paul. I thought about you when I went to bed last night, and wondered if we—Oliver and Austin and Elva and I—could have done anything to stop you. From marrying him, I mean.'

'Nobody could have stopped me.'

'Were you so much in love?'

Jeanne did not reply. She had long ago faced the fact that in marrying, she had been driven less by passion than by a longing to find security. Her father's long illness, following on his financial collapse, had shaken her. The alternatives at his death were to resume her teacher's training—or marry Paul Brisson. It had been easy to convince herself that she was in love with him. His patience with her father, his kindness to herself had built up in her complete confidence in a future spent with him. He had loved her—in his way. He still

45

loved her—in his way. But they had not found happiness together, and she had not found what she most longed for: a home.

'What happened?' Roberta broke into her reverie. 'Begin from where you left Rocksea. You went with your father to Canada. Et cetera.'

'He was in the hotel business. He'd been successful in France, but in Canada, I don't know why, he never got on to his feet. Things were bad, and then they got worse, and then he became ill. There was very little money—we found a cheap apartment in Quebec. There was no nursing for me to do—just looking after him and cooking, and being with him as much as possible. He hated to be left alone.

'It was just before he died that I met Paul again. We met in the street—I'd been shopping and I was carrying a basket full of vegetables. He'd just come back from Africa—he'd been on a shooting trip, and he told me a little about it and I thought it was wonderful, and he looked wonderful too, tough and tanned and different from any other man I'd met. He came to see us in the apartment, and he was so kind . . . I couldn't go out with him, so sometimes he used to bring food, and I'd cook it and we'd all have supper together. He was very patient with my father. And then my father went into hospital, and when he died, Paul asked me to marry him. So I did.'

'Pity.'

46

'It could have worked. It was my fault that it went wrong. He told me clearly what kind of life we would lead. He said frankly that he wasn't a domestic animal. He said he was like the animals he hunted—used to being free and hoping to remain free. He wasn't worried about me because he knew I was physically tough and could go on safari with him and keep up and not get in the way. It seemed to me a wonderful life—looking forward, I mean. Travelling to far-off places, camping, seeing beautiful, wild country . . . So I went with him. India, Africa, Brazil . . . and after a few months, I couldn't stand it any more.'

'Stand Paul?'

'No. The . . . the slaughter. The end of every trip was a row of beautiful animals, or birds, or fish, laid out—dead. Death. Killing. Killing on the hills, on the sea, in the jungle. Beaters and guns and rods, and money poured out to go somewhere else and find something more to kill. I stood it as long as I could. I tried to make him see my point of view, but you can't talk to a hunter about destruction. He'll tell you that man was always a hunting animal, hunting for food, killing in self-defence. Now it's all in the sacred name of sport. Paul called it the Hemingway life-style. Do you know what that means?'

'I know where it ends.'

'I hadn't any feeling about blood sports before I married him—but looking back now, all I can see is death.'

'So you decided to get out?'

'Not for that. I told myself that he was just what he'd been when we married, and I should have seen how things would turn out. And if I couldn't stand it, I should let him go on trips while I stayed at home with his aunts. It wasn't the hunting that finished everything. It was the twins.'

'Ah. What did he say when you told him you were pregnant?'

'Not much. He said it was a pity I couldn't go on trips with him. But that meant almost total separation—months on end, and then a short time at home, and then away again. And each time he came back, home meant less to him. Perhaps if the twins had been boys, he might have felt some kind of interest. But he's what he is, and he'll never change. I was crazy to think that the sight of children—his own children growing up—would turn him from a hunter into a parent. So at last we ended it, and when I got my divorce, I couldn't think of anywhere to go except France. And then your telegram came. Why were you all so sure it wouldn't work?'

'Well, take your character, and his. People don't have to be alike to get on, but there has to be something that can link up. You said just now that he isn't a domestic animal, and that's just what you are. Everything about you used to be, and as far as I can see still is geared to

48

the home. Going into the kitchen this morning, seeing you with those children, it hit me—children with their faces washed, their hair brushed, Mother neat, table with a cloth on it—I didn't know there was a cloth in the cottage—simple breakfast nicely set out. Order. That's something you won't find round me or round Elva. Either one of us would have suited Paul better, because neither of us ever had or ever wanted any moorings. I would have painted the animals, alive or dead, and Elva would have made notes on jungle flora and fauna.'

'You both liked Parson's House just because it was a home.'

'We were children, and it was nice to feel wanted. I'm sorry things didn't work out for you, but you've come out of it with a couple of nice children. Could you live permanently in England?'

'You mean would I like to? Yes. But it wouldn't be a sensible thing to do. In France, at least I'm at home; I've got relations there, even if I don't know them very well.'

'Well, at least you won't have to worry about money.'

'Your parents were separated, weren't they? Did they ever get divorced?'

'No, and never will. They've got a better idea. They have their shall-we-call-them-attachments, and when they get tired of them, they sigh and say what a pity it is that my

49

husband, or alternately my wife, will never agree to a divorce. That way, they get all the fun, and dodge the pay-off. And so to the next affair.'

'Do you ever see them?'

'If they come to England, they let me know—but that's about every three years. No hard feelings. I could never see why producing children should turn the producers into model parents. They live their lives, I live mine. I like being on my own. So does Elva. But you're different. You need a nest, and soon, some man or other will provide one.'

Jeanne smiled.

'We'll see,' she said, and rose. 'Time to go home.'

'Not straight home. I'm going to take you to see the Spice Box.'

It was not far away, a small shop on the corner of a street that led off the square.

'Leave the twins,' Roberta said. 'We won't be more than a few minutes.'

The outside of the shop was painted a brilliant Chinese red. In the window facing them as they got out of the car, Jeanne saw coloured photographs placed on stands—pictures showing some of the plants from which the spices were obtained—cinnamon, pimento, clove, myrtle, ginger, nutmeg. The window on the other corner was given up to a display of jars and dishes containing ground spices. Following Roberta into the sunny,

50

scented interior, Jeanne saw seated at a cash desk near the door a venerable old man, dark-skinned, white-haired, white-whiskered, with a long, mournful face. Behind the counter were two very different figures—a young Indian and a younger, enchantingly pretty girl with enormous black eyes, a smooth brown skin and oiled hair parted in the middle and worn in a coil on the nape of her neck. She grinned delightedly at the sight of Roberta. Her husband placed his palms together and gave the half-eastern, half-western bow he reserved for old customers.

'Jeanne, this is Suni,' Roberta said, 'and this is his wife Suji. Those aren't their real names, but they're the nearest anyone in Rocksea can get to the right pronunciation. This is Madame Brisson, from Canada, who's staying at the cottage with me. Jeanne, this is Grandfather.'

Grandfather, solemnly chewing a clove of garlic, rose and bowed.

'Welcome to our shop,' he said.

The success of the Spice Box was directly due to the house-to-house advertising campaign carried out by Suni and Suji shortly after it opened. Suni's English was not, like his grandfather's, fluent; his wife's was almost non-existent—but their message was clear enough. The pair appeared—smiling, eager, optimistic—on the doorsteps of astonished housewives, and Suni extolled the virtues of

51

curry as a health food. Curries, Suni explained, were rich in vitamins. Curries should be made in the eastern way in all western houses. The spices that went to their making had antiseptic value. Paprika and chili, ginger, turmeric, coriander, cinnamon, cardamom—Suni unrolled a parchment and displayed the list—were highly beneficial. Whenever he paused for breath, his wife interpolated an emphatic 'Oh yess, oh verrie good, yess.'

Only the most hardened housewives could resist this combination. Before long, hungry husbands came home ready to sit down to steak and kidney pies, and found themselves presented with Khari Moorghi, Hara Mircha or Anda Jheenga. The shop became a meeting place for the initiated. Off broad Devon tongues rolled requests for eelachie, dhunnia, udruck or kush-kush. The Spice Box set a fashion which spread beyond the confines of Rocksea.

In the social field, the family showed a complete reversal of these publicity methods. They paid no visits and issued no invitations. They were never seen in the garden, which being nothing but boulder and scrub, needed no attention. From back windows there fluttered on washing days endless lengths of spotless white material which Rocksea took to be sheets or saris or dhotis. The only sounds heard by the inmates of Vistamar, next door, were the slow, sad notes of Grandfather's flute.

Nobody knew how the family lived. Those who called in the hope of finding out, got no farther than the front door.

Jeanne, on this first visit to the shop, found Suni and Suji looking past her to watch the twins, who were peering through the windows of the car. Suni begged leave to bring them in. Suji lifted them on to the counter and let them play with her thin, silver, jingling bracelets. There could be no verbal communication between them, but none seemed needed. Grandfather, looking on, nodded his head indulgently and said that the lady was fortunate to have such pretty little girls, but would in time, he hoped, give birth to many handsome sons. This was his sole contribution until the visitors were leaving, when he rose and said some words in a low voice to Suni. Suni, with an exclamation, gave himself a blow on the forehead with his fist.

'Excuse, please,' he begged Roberta. 'When I saw you and this lady and the little children, everything went from my head. I did not speak of the rumours, to ask you what you are thinking.'

'Rumours?' Roberta sounded mystified, and Suni looked for enlightenment to his grandfather.

'I said the wrong word?' he asked.

'No. You were right. Rumours. Perhaps the lady has not heard them.'

'What rumours?' Roberta asked.

53

'Well, what they are saying,' Suni began eagerly, 'is—'

'No!' A stern command from his grandfather stopped him. 'It is permissible to speak of rumours to those who have heard them. But to begin them, to spread them—this is bad.'

'But they must have heard!' Suni protested. 'Everybody is talking, isn't it? And they live next door, how is it they didn't see that the workmen were less and even less?'

'They will learn in time,' Grandfather said.

'But they have been to the shops,' Suni persisted, 'and in all the shops people are saying this and that. Listen how our customers speak about it when they come. Everybody is saying.'

'I haven't been here long, and Madame Brisson only arrived last night,' Roberta explained.

'But it is very funny that somebody has not informed you,' Suni said. 'When you hear, please to let us know what you are thinking of it. I am not believing anything, but my grandfather is believing.'

'What do you think all that was about?' Roberta asked as she and Jeanne drove homeward.

'I don't know. They said the workmen had left, or were leaving, but they must still be there. I saw the scaffolding when we came out this morning.'

54

'The scaffolding's there, but now I come to think of it, the workmen aren't. When I first came down to the cottage, they were up there every day with ladders and pots of paint, but they don't seem to be there now.'

'On strike?'

'Probably.'

When they reached the cottage, Jeanne prepared a picnic lunch. It was no ham-sandwich affair; she packed into the basket a variety of cold foods, added fruit and then made a flask of hot coffee. Roberta looked in to enquire what was being taken down in the way of drink.

'Milk for the twins,' Jeanne told her. 'That's all they like drinking—milk, milk, milk. They hate juices of any kind.'

'So do I. And I don't want milk, milk, milk. You and I are going to share a bottle of wine. You'll find some bottles up on that shelf. I don't know whether Oliver left them for us as a nice welcoming touch, but if he didn't, he should have done. I've already got through . . .' She paused, frowning in annoyance. 'Now who could that be?'

Someone was knocking at the front door, which was on the other side of the house. Roberta glanced out of one of the windows and raised her voice to a shout.

'Would you mind coming round to this side?—One of the workmen, I think,' she told Jeanne as they waited. 'You can slip out with

55

the twins if you want to, and I'll join you later.'

When she opened the door, they saw a short, stout, florid, balding man dressed in a check jacket, an open shirt and corduroy trousers, a tweed cap in his hand. He spoke in strong Cockney tones.

'Morning, miss. Sorry to trouble you. Shan't keep you long. The name's Quinter. Don't suppose you know the firm. Builders. Quinter and Co. We haven't been in Rocksea long, but you may 'ave noticed our sign on the 'ouse next door. Can I 'ave a word with you, if it's convenient?'

'Come in,' Roberta invited.

'Thanks. Those your kids outside?' he enquired, entering. 'If so, I shouldn't be callin' you miss.'

'They belong to Madame Brisson, a friend of mine.'

Mr Quinter pressed his cap to his stomach and bowed.

'Nice kids,' he told Jeanne. 'You don't often see 'em identical, like that.'

'Sit down,' Roberta invited. 'We were just going off for a beach picnic, but there's time for coffee, or a drink. Which?'

'No, really,' protested Mr Quinter. 'I wouldn't like to—'

'There's beer in the fridge.'

'Then you've got a customer. Thanks a lot, miss. I was pleased when I saw the sun after all that rain we've been 'aving, but I don't take to

56

heat much.' He looked at Jeanne.

'Don't want to seem nosey, but Madame . . . French, would you be?' he asked.

'Yes. The twins are French-Canadian.'

'Ah. Do you speak French when you're at 'ome?'

'Yes. We're from the province of Quebec,' Jeanne explained. 'French is spoken in the home and in the schools.'

'That's what I thought,' said Mr Quinter. 'I 'ad a friend, more of a business colleague as you might say, and 'e joined an English firm in Quebec and he told me they 'ad to change the letter-'eads on the firm's paper, so's to include French names and whatnot. He said they didn't 'ave no choice; they had to do it, or get out. So they did it. Lot of nationalism going about these days. Oh—thank you, miss.'

He took the glass of beer Roberta handed him, drank, ran his tongue appreciatively over his lips, and placed the glass on the table.

'What can we do for you, Mr Quinter?' she asked.

'I don't know as you can do anything, miss. If there was anything concrete . . . but there isn't. It's all like wool—cotton wool. Nothing to get your teeth into, nothing to catch 'old of. I tried—'

'This wouldn't be connected with certain rumours, by any chance?'

'What else, miss?' There was a hopeless note in his voice. 'The shops are full of 'em.

The pub's full of 'em. They don't talk of nothing else at the Lion, and—'

'One moment.' Roberta stopped him. 'We only heard there were rumours. Nobody told us what the rumours were. All we know is that they're connected with the house next door.'

Mr Quinter's pale blue eyes grew round.

'You mean you 'aven't 'eard what—'

'I haven't been here long, and Madame Brisson only arrived last night.'

'Then that accounts for it. Well, I'll tell you. If you don't mind, I'll go back a bit and remind you that we're a new firm in Rocksea. This job—the job I contracted to do next door, at what they call Parson's House, was my first, as you might say, bite. So naturally I was keen to make a go of it. So I got my men on to it, doing—'

'Doing what exactly?' Jeanne asked. 'Decorating?'

'Not only decorating, miss, madame. There was to be an extra bathroom, and glassing-in the balconies and a complete going-over, inside and out. Mr Selby came down from London and went over the 'ouse with me. Have you ever met the gentleman?'

'No. We knew his brother, Mr David Selby,' Roberta said.

'He was a different sort, they tell me. I'm not sayin' anything against Mr Maurice Selby, only that he's not an easy man to work for. He told me exactly 'ow he wanted the house done,

58

and then 'e went back to London and we started on the job, and the next thing you know, the trouble started. And as much as I did me best to say it was all rubbish, the rumours spread and the men began to drop off and—'

'Drop off why?' Roberta asked.

'Because . . .' Mr Quinter stopped, reached for his glass and drained it. He shook his head when Roberta moved to open another bottle. 'No, thanks all the same, miss. One's my limit on a 'ot morning. And things are mixed-up enough as it is; I've got to keep a clear 'ead if I can, with all this going on.'

'What *is* going on?' Roberta enquired.

'The job isn't,' Mr Quinter said dejectedly. 'There was no use trying to carry on with 'arf a work force, and the other 'arf getting ready to go. I called a halt. I went to London and I put the matter in front of Mr Selby. I got what I expected to get. I got what I daresay I'd have given another chap if he'd come to me with a fairy tale and expected me to swallow it. Mr Selby said if I couldn't keep hysteria out of the ranks—his own words, miss—he'd find somebody else who could. He gave me one week to get the men back on the job, and a month to complete it. How can I complete a job if I can't get men to work on it? So I was going to chuck the thing up—and a nice start that would've been to getting the firm's feet on the ground in Rocksea. This is a growing place,

59

a place any builder can do well in. But I couldn't see any way out of this turn-up—until last night, when my wife woke me up and said why didn't I go along and see the lady who's rented the cottage next door to Parson's House? Because she'd 'eard you used to live at Parson's House some years back, and she said you'd be able to tell me if there was any of this funny business going on when you lived there. So that's why I came—to ask you.'

'Madame Brisson and I used to spend our school holidays there,' Roberta told him. 'But we can't help you if you don't tell us what the funny business is.'

Mr Quinter opened his mouth, closed it again, took a deep breath and brought out one word.

'Ghosts,' he said.

There was a pause.

'*Ghosts?*' repeated Jeanne.

'*Ghosts?*' echoed Roberta.

'That's right. Ghosts. Spooks.'

'At Parson's House?' Roberta asked in a dazed voice.

'That's the size of it, miss. An' sitting 'ere looking at you two ladies, so sensible, so level-'eaded, I can 'ardly bring meself to talk about it. It makes me feel a fool. But facts are facts, and the facts are that since we started work on that house, chaps you'd have taken your oath were hard-headed, straight-thinking men, 'ave come to me and told me they weren't going

60

inside the place again. And the ones who laughed at them came to me later on with the same tales. I 'ave to believe them. What workman would throw up his job if 'e didn't 'ave strong reasons? They all told the same story: doors they'd shut tight, opening themselves. Windows the same. Rooms with nothin' but furniture in them, weren't as empty as they looked. And not one of them, before all this 'appened, would've believed in a ghost if you'd waved one in front of 'is nose. And even if you could explain what was happening among the men, you can't write off the cleaning woman's evidence.'

'What cleaning woman?' Jeanne asked.

'Name of Clermont. Mrs Clermont. She's been working there for years, and with the 'ouse empty, she's been acting as caretaker. She goes—'

'We know her,' Roberta said. 'She used to work at the house when we were there. Has she been seeing ghosts too?'

'She laughed louder than most at first, miss. Laughed right in the men's faces. Called them . . . well, we needn't go into that. And then, last Tuesday, she started 'er cleaning as usual—well, not as usual; all she was doing was keeping down the mess the men was making. And then . . .'

'And then?' prompted Jeanne.

'Well, I was in that little room they call the terrace room, the—'

61

'Yes, we know. Go on,' Jeanne said.

'I was in there payin' off the men who wanted to leave the job. We all saw Mrs Clermont giving the 'all a sweep—she's got all the furniture covered up under dust sheets. Then she went up the stairs. And a few minutes later, there was a clatter, such a clatter as I couldn't describe to you, and we all got into the 'all and there was Mrs Clermont coming tumbling down the stairs, broom and bucket and all. I got to the bottom stair before she did, so she fell soft, but she was in a bad state. Like death, she was, and couldn't speak at first. Then she said there was something in the way when she wanted to get up the second flight of stairs. She couldn't see anything, but she said she could *feel* something. She thought she was in for one of 'er dizzy spells, so she turned to come downstairs—and she said something touched 'er on the shoulder. And she took the rest of the stairs in one. So there you are. You can make your own minds up. Mr Selby said that once these rumours got round, people let their imaginations run riot. Well, I'm not saying 'e isn't right, but he didn't see Mrs Clermont when I got 'er right side up.'

'Did you . . .' Jeanne paused, and Mr Quinter finished the question.

'Did I go upstairs and take a look? Yes, miss, madame, I did. It took nerve, I can tell you, though I shouldn't give myself the credit. I

62

went straight upstairs and across that sort of gallery on the upper floor. Nothing. Nothing to see, nothing to feel. I took a good grip of the banisters on the way down, but nothing touched me. But I must have shown something on my face, because there wasn't one of 'em there who didn't think I was holding something back. All I'll tell you, which I didn't tell them, was that a window at the end of the gallery was open, and I knew none of my men 'ad opened it, and I didn't think it likely that Mrs Clermont 'ad, either. I was afraid to ask, in case I didn't like the answer. Apart from that, nothing.'

Nobody spoke for a time. Then Roberta put a question.

'Have all the men left the job?'

'All except one—my partner. He's a religious chap and 'e belongs to one of those societies that believe you can't be hurt if you think the right way. He's up there now, working on 'is own. What can I do with one workman? Was there any trouble like this when you lived there?'

'No. And I wouldn't have thought,' Roberta said, 'that Parson's House was the kind of house a ghost would choose to haunt.'

'That's the first thing I said, miss. I've seen a lot of houses in my time, but I never saw one with more light, more sun—when the sun was shining—more out-looking, if I can put it that way. Not a dark corner in the whole place. I

63

don't know what the furniture's like, because it's all covered up, but those rooms are lovely, there's no other word. You know what I did yesterday? I went to the public library and I looked up ghosts—and those other things. Pol . . .'

'Poltergeists?'

'That's it. Poltergeists. It said they make a lot of noise and shove furniture about. But the furniture 'asn't moved and there's no noises anywhere. If it wasn't going on in your time, then why—'

'Could we go up there now?' Roberta asked him.

He stared at her in surprise.

'Go up to the house?' He paused to consider the suggestion. 'It mightn't be a bad idea. If I could say you'd both been round the place with me, and nothing happened, that could be something I could use next time someone talked to me about ghosts. Would you come, then?'

Roberta went to the door and called to the twins, who were making mud pies in preparation for making them of sand.

'We're going up to see that big house,' she told them, 'where your Mummy and I lived when we were little girls. Then we'll go to the beach and have our picnic. Come on; you can come too.'

They went up to the house by the steep path that the holiday children had helped to make

64

so that they could get from cottage to house without going out into the road. When they reached the small wooden gate at the top, Mr Quinter paused.

'I ought to tell you,' he said, 'that one of my orders was to remove this.'

'The gate?' Jeanne asked.

'Yes. And put up a low wall along here. You needn't mind much; from what I saw of Mrs Selby, she isn't going to be a friendly neighbour you'd want to pop over and see very often.'

Jeanne and Roberta scarcely heard him; they were looking at the garden. None of the other four houses on the promontory had much more than a strip of scrub surrounding them, but there had been enough space in front of Parson's House for a garden made of flagged terraces, hardy shrubs and a picturesque little pool set among stones. Roberta walked to the edge of the property and gazed down at the beach.

'How often did we race the boys down these steps?' she asked. She turned to look at the house. 'It's absurd to imagine ghosts here.'

'Or anywhere,' Jeanne said. 'But you believe in them.'

'You do, miss?' Mr Quinter asked, amazed.

'I only believe in my own ghosts, not in other people's,' Roberta told him, 'and I certainly don't believe there's anything here but what Mr Selby called mass hysteria. Which way shall we go in?'

'We'll go in this way, as it's open. Mind the scaffolding,' Mr Quinter warned them, and stopped to introduce a man even stouter than himself who, at the top of a ladder, was painting the lamp over the back door. 'My partner, Mr Bert Inskip. The only chap in the firm who doesn't scare easy. Bert, these ladies used to live in this 'ouse, so they're going in to see what it's all about.'

'Morning,' Bert said cheerfully. 'There'll be some more workmen along in a day or two— I've got hold of my uncle in Exeter and asked him to send over some of his chaps. We'll make a new start.'

'Maybe.' Mr Quinter sounded sceptical. 'Will you go round on your own, ladies, or do you want me to go with you?'

'Alone, I think,' Roberta said. 'Come on, Jeanne. Come on, twins.'

They walked through to the front of the house and stood looking round at the shrouded furniture. Through the wide windows they could see the expanse of sea. Going slowly through the rooms, Jeanne thought that what had impressed their youthful minds had been the graciousness, the spaciousness of the house, and the freedom that they were allowed within it. Such restrictions as there had been were sensible and not frustrating; indoors and out there had been the feeling that they were not strangers, not visitors, but part of the

66

family.

They went through the kitchen and to the stone-floored room which Austin Parkes had christened the Clean-Up, as it was here that they entered from the garden and left their muddy boots, hung their damp or dirty outdoor garments and washed their hands.

They went upstairs and along the gallery, and looked into the bedrooms opening off it. They climbed up to the great, bare room at the top of the house—the playroom they had seldom used, since indoor games had been more fun played down at the cottage.

'Look.' Roberta called to them from her old bedroom. 'You can still climb out on to that branch. Remember when we did Romeo and Juliet, and Paul fell off in the middle of his big speech?'

'He didn't fall off,' Jeanne said. 'Austin sawed the branch and it snapped off.'

Roberta stared at her in amazement.

'Austin did that? Why?'

'Because you were Juliet and he thought he should have been Romeo. But you chose Paul.'

'Naturally. He looked like Romeo. Why didn't Austin arrange it so that I was the one who fell on the flagstones? And how is it you know about it, and the rest of us didn't?'

'I only found out because I was puzzled, and went and looked at the branch later.'

'But you didn't give Austin away.'

'No. It was such a silly trick. I didn't want

anybody to know about it.'

'Paul would have mashed him up.'

'I know. So I kept quiet.'

They went downstairs and joined Mr Quinter outside the house.

'Anything?' he asked.

'Nothing,' Jeanne answered.

'Nothing at all,' Roberta corroborated.

'Well, that's two,' Mr Quinter said. 'With me and my wife and Bert and Mr and Mrs Selby, there's seven against the rumour-spreaders.'

As they passed the ladder, Bert spoke to them.

'Did you say you ladies lived here once?' he asked.

Roberta looked up.

'We used to come for school holidays,' she told him. 'For about five years. And I've been coming ever since—on and off.'

'Then you'd know if anything ever happened in the house—like a tragedy, somebody doing somebody in, something like that. That's where ghosts go, if they go—to a place where there's been dirty deeds done. Did anything like that ever happen in this house?'

'No. It was built by Mrs David Selby's father,' Jeanne said. 'He was a parson and he sold it to old Mr Selby, who left it to his elder son, Maurice. There was a quarrel when Mr David Selby married, but it was just a family quarrel. David and his wife lived here, and the brother, Maurice, went to London.'

68

'And David died quietly in his bed, and his wife died while she was on a cruise, and was buried at sea,' added Roberta.

'Nothing for ghosts there,' Bert commented. 'Myself, I put it down to all these rumours. The people in Rocksea strike me as being a thick-headed lot. You wouldn't get Londoners going round yapping about ghosts. Do you want my real opinion of all this upset?'

His listeners indicated that they would.

'What I think is that someone's picked on this way of getting their own back on this Mr Selby, who owns the house. From what I hear of him, he's never been popular, and they say he's played a few dirty tricks on the business people round about here. I'll bet you that somebody who doesn't like him has found out that he's coming back here to live permanent, and intending to occupy this house once we've done it up for him. What's easier than for them to say to themselves: I'll see to it that nobody gets his house ready for him; I'll put a rumour-bomb in the town, and when it goes off, it'll scare everybody and turn the house into a haunt. If I'd thought of the idea myself, I'd have said it was too silly to work—but it's worked, hasn't it? It's worked a treat. Maybe we've only seen the start of it. It might be a long time before Mr Selby gets comfortably into his house—if he gets into it at all.'

He turned back to his work, and Mr Quinter followed Jeanne and Roberta and the

69

twins to the short cut.

'My car's outside your gate,' he said. 'I'm sorry I've taken up so much of your time. I'll tell my wife—'

He stopped. From above had come the sound of a crash and a loud cry. The cry was followed by shouts for help, uttered in Bert's voice.

Mr Quinter set the pace on the way back, with Jeanne and Roberta close behind him and the twins panting in the rear, their tin pails clattering against the rocks as they came. They found Bert lying by the ladder. As they bent over him, he struggled to rise.

'You 'urt, Bert?' Mr Quinter asked anxiously.

'Yes. No. I'm alive, anyhow. Get me up, will you?'

They helped him to his feet. His face, which they had a few minutes before seen cheerful, tight-cheeked and florid, was pallid and seemed to have shrunk.

''Ow did you manage to fall off?' Mr Quinter asked in bewilderment.

Bert, steadying himself, raised his head slowly and looked upward. Following his glance, they saw nothing but the lamp on which he had been working, and above it, open window shutters.

'I didn't fall,' he said. 'I mean, I didn't fall by myself. It was those shutters did it. Who the blazes opened them?'

Mr Quinter turned to Jeanne and Roberta, but Bert spoke again, this time in a voice of decision.

'Never mind asking them,' he told Mr Quinter. 'Those shutters came open with a bang, and one of them caught me a clout on the side of the head and knocked me clean off the ladder. If I wasn't so well padded, I'd have broken a few bones. When shutters blow open in a gale, that's one thing. When they fly out with the force that those did, when there isn't a breath of wind, it makes you think. So what I think is that I'm going to give this ghost best. I'm not going to say I've changed my mind. I'm not for, and I'm not against; all I know is that I'm not going to bring any chaps over to work on a job that's piled up the casualties the way this job has. I don't know what's going on, and I'm not going to stop to find out. You'd better stay with me for a bit,' he told Mr Quinter, 'just till I feel my legs steady again.'

Back at the cottage, Jeanne and Roberta made no reference to the incident until they were carrying the picnic basket down to the beach. Then Roberta put a question.

'Did we open that window?'

'No, we didn't.'

'Then—?'

'Someone else presumably did. I suppose you believe that it opened itself and pushed Bert off the ladder?'

'Well, funnily enough, no. You thought I was

71

going to say yes, didn't you?'

'I thought you'd want company for your London friend.'

'If there's a ghost at Parson's House, it'll have to do something more impressive than scaring a few builders and cleaning women before I take it seriously. I don't expect you to believe in my ghost. If you investigated, you'd say it was the way the studio curtain caught the light and sent a shadow on to the bed. I know it isn't, but I wouldn't try to convince anybody else.'

'At least you *see* your ghost. I'd rather see one than feel one.'

They had reached the beach. Jeanne put the basket in the shade of a small rock. Roberta was looking up at Parson's House, and after a time she spoke thoughtfully.

'If there was a ghost up there,' she said, 'it would be a gentle ghost. The parson, his wife, his daughter Lorna, David. All so much a part of the house that nobody could be surprised if they came back to it. But if they did, they wouldn't push anybody downstairs and they wouldn't push anybody off ladders.'

'So no ghost?'

'No ghost,' Roberta said decisively.

CHAPTER THREE

Their first day on an English beach left the twins determined to return to it as soon as possible and stay on it as long as possible. They were up at dawn on the following morning, and Jeanne found them in the kitchen preparing their breakfast. She removed the bread knife from Jo's grasp, closed the refrigerator, wiped up pools of milk, washed honey from Polly's fingers and lifted both children on to their chairs.

'What's the big hurry this morning?' she enquired.

'We're going to the beach, to play.' Polly sounded calm, but determined. Jeanne recognised the tone. Slow at making up her mind, Polly could seldom be induced to change it.

'Wif our buckets,' Jo said. 'We can go by ourselfs.'

'No, you can't. Remember that,' Jeanne said. 'I'll take you whenever I can, which is most of the time—but if I can't take you or some other grown-up can't take you, you wait until we can. Understand?'

Apparently not. Polly broke the rebellious silence.

'We can see the way.'

'If we swim by ourselfs,' supplemented Jo,

73

'we don't get drowned. Yesterday, you saw.'

'All the same, someone's got to be with you,' Jeanne said firmly. 'When you're bigger, you can go by yourselves. And if you open a fridge, close it again or the ice will melt and everything will get warm. And don't have breakfast in your pyjamas; you've spilt milk all down your fronts. When you've had breakfast, you can get into your swim suits and go outside and play, and as soon as I've made the picnic, we'll go down to the beach.'

She finished dressing before she prepared her own breakfast. Roberta came down as she was making coffee, and sat watching her. It was by now clear that Roberta was by nature disposed to sit and watch while others worked, and to this Jeanne had no objection, for she had come to the conclusion that if order was to be established in the cottage, she herself would have to be the one who established it.

Filling Roberta's cup and handing it to her, she raised the subject.

'About the house,' she said. 'I would like to do the housekeeping. Is that all right with you?'

'And with Elva too, if housekeeping means doing the cooking and the cleaning and the shopping too. But you can't do it alone. Why not get old Mrs Clermont to help you, if she's recovered from her somersault down the stairs? She's on Oliver's payroll. He pays her by the month—she acts as caretaker when the

74

cottage is empty. She'd come if you asked her to. I told Oliver I didn't want her, but—'

'I don't want her, either. If you and Elva will look after the rooms upstairs, I'll do the ones down here. Shopping is no trouble. Cooking . . . I like cooking. But I would like to make a rule.'

'Go ahead.'

'I like to see people sitting round a table at meal times. Nobody sits down now the way they used to, and—'

'It's such a deadly waste of time. If I feel hungry, I open a can or take something out of the fridge.'

'I know. Yesterday you took the children's supper.'

'I did?'

'You did. In future, I'll label what is for you and for Elva, and nobody will touch the rest.'

'That's all right—so long as it's all as good as the children's supper was. What was the rule you were going to make?'

'Dinner. Fix any time you like. The twins will be in bed. I would like you to say eight, half-past eight, even nine, but when I call you at that time, you come and sit down in a proper way to have a proper meal.'

'Make it eight-thirty. We'll put on clean collars and eat off Lorna's best china and we'll use knives and forks and we won't throw bones over our shoulders. So that's settled. You feed us and keep us clean. We do our own work and appear in time for dinner.' She reached for the coffee pot and refilled her cup and Jeanne's. 'Did you dream of ghosts?'

'No. Before I believe in this ghost, it will have to push me downstairs. I don't—'

She broke off as a crash sounded outside. She was on her feet and at the door in a moment, Roberta not far behind her.

What they saw on emerging from the house was a step-ladder lying on its side. Beside it was an upturned bucket. Jo was getting slowly to her feet. Polly was standing by, watching but making no attempt to help her.

'Why don't you help your sister when she falls down?' Jeanne asked in amazement. 'And what are you doing with this step-ladder?'

'Which came,' Roberta said, 'from the garage. How in the world did they manage to carry it?'

'It wasn't my fault.' Polly spoke calmly. 'I said she could be the other man, but she said no, she wanted to be the fat man on the ladder, so she climbed up it and then—'

'She pushed me!'

'I did not push you. I pushed only the ladder. If you were that man, you had to fall off, didn't you? Didn't she, Maman? Like he fell off.'

'Pushing ladders when your sister's on them doesn't sound to me like a game,' Jeanne said. 'Why couldn't she pretend to fall off?'

'Because he fell off really,' Polly explained.

76

'Who'd have children?' Roberta asked, as she and Jeanne went back to their coffee. 'When I first saw yours, I thought maybe I'd missed something, but not any more. Our parents knew what they were doing when they farmed us out for holidays. Do you want me to help you with the lunch?'

'No, thank you. Are you eating on the beach with us?'

'Yes.'

'Then I'll make some extra.'

Clearing away the breakfast things, she felt a sense of relief; if she was left to take care of these rooms downstairs, all would be well. Upstairs would not be her concern, though how Roberta could exist, let alone work in the disorder that had met her eyes when she had been taken up to see the studio, passed her comprehension. Frames, canvas, tiles, paint, unmade bed, jars of cosmetics here and there, clothes everywhere. And from this chaos, she thought with wonder, Roberta emerged looking fresh and groomed and lovely.

She drove with the twins to the supermarket and stocked up with provisions she had not listed the day before, including fish and meat. When they were back at the cottage, she put the children outside to play while she prepared a picnic lunch and did the preliminary work for dinner. Throughout the rest of the day she stayed with the children on the beach; when they came up to the cottage, she gave the children their supper, put them into bed and left them to look at picture books for the permitted half hour. In the kitchen, she finished the preparations for dinner, and with a view to giving herself more elbow-room in which to work, as well as a little more peace, she moved out of the kitchen the easy chairs which had been taken from the sitting room. These she grouped round the small table, so that Roberta and Elva could sit drinking aperitifs before dinner, close enough to enable her to be sociable, but not close enough to get in her way.

The weather continued fine. They breakfasted morning after morning with the sun streaming into the kitchen. They passed quiet, happy days on the beach. Roberta joined them when she wanted to, appearing in a beach robe which consisted of two artistically-draped scarves which every day seemed to become smaller and more wispy, until it seemed to Jeanne that they must soon reach vanishing point.

The peace extended to the house next door. No workmen were to be seen. The scaffolding had been removed, the board bearing the name of Mr Quinter's firm had been carried away. If rumours of ghosts were still going round the town, Jeanne and Roberta did not hear them, but there was evidence enough that interest in the supernatural was still active, for knots of spectators gathered daily to stand staring at Parson's House.

One morning Jeanne had a suggestion to make.

'If I could trust you to keep an eye on the twins,' she said to Roberta, 'I'd leave them with you and take back that hired car. I wouldn't be gone long.'

'Why wouldn't you trust me?'

'You'd go upstairs and get interested in your painting and I'd come home and find the children floating across to France.'

'Leave them with me and tell Polly to keep an eye on me. She's quite up to seeing I don't forget them.'

'You promise not to go upstairs and work?'

'I swear.'

'And you promise not to go into a dream and forget them?'

'Cross my heart.'

'Then I'll go. I'll get the lunch basket ready for you to take down to the beach. Don't let the twins eat before I get back.'

'What about me?'

'Keep the basket closed until I come.'

Settled with the children on the beach, Roberta thought that on a morning like this, anybody might be forgiven for dreaming. The sun was almost too hot, the sea was mirror-smooth, the sky clear, with an occasional fleecy cloud to break the expanse of blue. They had the beach to themselves. The twins had found a pool and were making a wide-spreading

79

and complicated series of fortifications round it. A good-looking pair, she thought; hard to tell, at this stage, what they would look like when they were grown up, but they were well worth looking at now.

The man coming down the path from the cottage, in bathing trunks with a towel slung over his shoulder, had the same thought, but he was not thinking of the twins. His eyes were on Roberta, lying stretched on the sand, and he took in her slender, almost naked body and long, lovely limbs and felt, as he always felt on seeing her after an interval, the familiar pangs of mingled desire and despair. She didn't want him; she had told him so more than once. But he was optimistic by nature, and he told himself that it would be all right if he went on working at it. It wouldn't do to hurry her; the girl had only known him for fifteen years.

The children, staring, brought Roberta's glance to him. She sat up and spoke in astonishment.

'Austin!'

He came unhurriedly the rest of the way, dropped on to the sand beside her and dropped a light kiss on her palm.

'How's things?' he asked.

It occurred to her, as she looked at him, that he had changed little since she had first seen him—which had been on this beach. Tall, lean, gangling, he had thick, untidy brown hair, sleepy grey eyes, a long nose and a jutting chin.

80

Nobody had ever called him handsome, but he was a man liked by almost everyone who knew him. He had irrepressible spirits; his presence was a stimulant to all but the most soured. Wealthy, he showed little interest in money and had never in his life looked at a financial paper. His boyhood's ambition—to use for charitable purposes an inheritance which he felt to be the fruits of exploitation—was being achieved without any trouble on his part, since he left details and decisions to Oliver Hobart. His pet scheme, homes in which those in the lower income groups could live in a way that was a compromise between the private and the communal, was meeting with marked success. Life, he thought, was good, and would be perfect if the woman he loved, loved him.

'Lovely to see you,' he said, and eyed her scarves. 'I like your new two-piece.'

'I thought you were in Spain.'

'Not Spain. Portugal. You ought to study the stamps on my letters, even though you don't bother to read the contents. I got back last night, picked up Oliver and drove down here. That's to say, to Exeter. He wanted to come the whole way, but I convinced him that 3 a.m. was no time to wake up sleeping tenants.'

'Where is he?'

'On his way. He picked up his car in Exeter and he's stopping in Hine to see a client. Where's Jeanne?'

'Gone to return a car she hired.'

81

'Nice children.' He rose, walked over to them, sat cross-legged on the sand in front of them and returned their unblinking stare. 'You see if you like me? I see if I like you,' he told them, and fell silent, gazing. After a time: 'Yes, I like you. What do they call you?'

To Roberta's surprise, he got an answer. Polly was even smiling.

'I'm Polly. Her's Jo. Maman's gone out.'

'So I hear. I knew your mother when she was a little girl. She was very, very naughty.'

'Naughty?' echoed Jo.

'Terribly. I'll tell you about it one day. Did you bring enough lunch for me?' he asked Roberta.

'No. If you'd taken the trouble to phone and say you were coming, we—'

'—would have put in another couple of bottles of wine.' He was examining the contents of the picnic basket. 'These look suspiciously like the ones Oliver put on a shelf out of reach—he thought.' He opened a package, selected a meat pie and bit into it. 'Missed breakfast,' he explained. 'I stopped on the way here and bought some things for our lunch, but when I got to the cottage, nobody. I looked down here, saw you, took off my clothes and joined you. Tell me about Jeanne. Has she changed?'

'Hardly at all. She's still very French.'

'End of descriptive account?'

'Well, she's more or less as you remember

82

her, but more so. Small, neat, pretty, well-organised. Sort of serene. Domesticated. In another ten years she's going to be one of those plump, well-groomed Frenchwomen you see in the Paris markets, looking very housewifely and efficient, buying cheap cuts of meat and taking home live lobsters. No fuss, no flapping, but things get done. I think she had a pretty miserable time with Paul on the whole, but she can still laugh.'

'Has her accent improved?'

'No. She'll never call a ship anything but a sheep, but her English is fluent.'

'How long is she going to stay?'

'As long as she wants to. She hasn't made any hard-and-fast plans.'

'She'll need time to sort herself out, I suppose.'

'She'll need a husband. She won't have any trouble finding one—there's something about her that makes you think of a candle-lit dining room and the children coming in in long nightgowns to kiss Papa good night. She would have made a wonderful nurse, but she's opted for a house, not a hospital. If ever there's a fire at the cottage, she'll get the twins out first and then she'll go back for the kitchen stove.'

'Any sign of missing Paul?'

'Not a single one.'

'He still writes, I see.'

'How do you know that?'

'Two fat letters on the doormat—Canadian

stamps.'

'It's all over—finished.'

'The fat letters being merely a postscript, I suppose? Is she going to settle down with you, or look for a place of her own?'

'She's going to stay at the cottage—why else did we ask her to come? It's going to work out nicely. She's taken over the shopping and the housework and the cooking.'

'Already? She sized you up pretty swiftly. What wrecked the marriage?'

'She said she couldn't stand the slaughter. Dead animals and birds and fishes, all so beautiful, laid out in rows, dead and done for.'

'Not all dead, surely? He makes a lot of money supplying zoos with live specimens. Did she have to be his safari or shikari partner? Couldn't she have stayed at home and looked after the twins?'

'He was away most of the time. Staying home, or going with him, I can see it wasn't much of a life. I'm surprised she stuck it for so long.'

'Did he kick at losing the children?'

'No. Far from. She seemed surprised that they didn't rouse his paternal instincts. I didn't tell her that most men I know don't exactly cheer at the thought of becoming fathers. But it's odd, her marriage not lasting. Wouldn't you have said that out of the six of us, she would have been the one you'd say was the most happy-ever-after type?'

84

'No, I wouldn't. Certainly not. I'd say that I was the one most likely to qualify. If you married me, I'd be happy ever after. So would you, once you got used to the idea.'

'Maybe. Where are you going to stay while you're here?'

'At Cristall's. Oliver and I have business in Rocksea that'll take some time.'

'Why can't he go and stay at Cristall's too?'

Austin's eyebrows went up.

'Oliver? Didn't you agree to let him use his room at the cottage?'

'Yes, I did, but he said use it sometimes, and I thought he meant sometimes. I didn't know he'd start using it before we'd got ourselves settled. Will you please stop eating the children's lunch?'

'Think of the replacements I brought: pâté, smoked salmon, avocados, a jar of baby pickled beetroots, curried prawns from the delicatessen, liver sausage, the kind Oliver likes—and a bottle of very special port from my late father's cellar. And you begrudge me these mouthfuls?'

'The stuff you brought won't be much use to the twins.'

'They'll love them. They've probably got an inborn sense of what's good to eat, being French. I suppose Jeanne will bring them up in France? That's a pity, in a way. Canada's where they belong.'

'Belong? Who belongs anywhere these

days? Every place in Europe looks to me just like everywhere else. Get off a plane, if you haven't been hi-jacked on the way, and three guesses won't tell you where you are, with no local customs and no local costumes and everybody wearing blue jeans, and the same pop records blaring, and the same silly faces on the cinema posters, and the same student demonstrations and protest meetings and hapless hostages and terrorists putting bombs under or into your car to blow up people to get other people out of prison, and robbing your money in stick-ups when you want to cash a cheque. So where's the difference where you belong, if you belong?'

She leaned across to close the picnic basket, and Austin rescued a slipping scarf.

'I didn't quite follow that impassioned speech,' he said, 'but if you're trying to say that nobody today has national affiliations, you're off course. The world's busy dividing itself into smaller and smaller sub-divisions, one-people, one-nation.'

'That's what the builder said.'

'Builder?'

'Mr Quinter. He said there was what he called a lot of nationalism going about.'

'He was right. Twice a week come ambassadors from newly-emerged or newly-recognised states, with newly-designed flags ready to flutter over newly-furnished Embassies. I'm thinking seriously of going in

86

for printing atlases, no sooner sold than out of date. But for the moment, I'm busy with my second Parkes project.'

'Another apartment block?'

'A nice, low one, like the first project. Three storeys, nobody marooned in the clouds. The Leeds one is a tremendous success. I'd show you the plans for the Rocksea one if I thought you could make head or tail.'

She gave him a long, puzzled look.

'You really think you're going to change the national way of life, don't you?' she asked.

'Going to? I already have.' He rolled his towel into a pillow, put it against a rock, leaned back and then leaned forward again to pull the picnic basket closer. 'Go up to Leeds and take a look. The families living in that block I built will never want to live any other way. Fifteen apartments for private living—but on the ground floor, a launderette and an ironing room, so that Mum can wash and iron without cluttering up the kitchen. Also a babies' crèche with attendant, also a television room, so Junior can do his homework without the telly screeching. The only mistake I made at Leeds was not adding a snack-bar. The Rocksea block's going to have one, non-profit-making. Am I boring you?'

'What do you care?'

'What I meant to say was: are you paying attention? What I did at Leeds was prove what nobody but myself had fully realised: that

87

people in this country don't take kindly to communal living, but welcome some basic communal amenities. Do you want that put into simpler language, or are you following me? I find it quite incredible that families have for so long been shutting themselves up in separate little cells. It all started when some incredible lunatic said that the Englishman's home was his castle, or vice versa. Being shut up in a castle is one thing. Cooking and washing and ironing on separate machines in millions of separate little homes all over the country is not only crazy, but wickedly wasteful, and I'm successfully demonstrating the fact.'

'You're going to be very popular with all the makers of all the unwanted millions of all the unwanted separate machines. And you're also going to be popular with Jeanne, because you've eaten her lunch, as well as mine and the twins'. Will you stop talking and take the twins for a swim?'

'It's much too soon after eating,' he protested. 'I'd sink like a stone. And I don't often get a chance like this, to see you alone, and I want to talk about our future. I don't want to want another fifteen years.'

'If you sink like a stone, you won't have to. Will you go and swim?'

'You take one twin, I'll take the other.'

'No. I'm going to sunbathe and wait for Jeanne. She'll be here on the next bus.'

When the next bus came in, Jeanne was not on it. Giving up the car had been a longer process than she had anticipated, for the girl in charge of the agent's office had displayed more self-assurance than efficiency. Only after a long delay, and with reluctance, had she admitted that she knew very little about the job and would have to call for help. Help arrived some time later in the form of a supercilious but better-informed young man—and Jeanne, looking at her watch, saw that if she wanted to catch the bus, she would have to run for it.

She saw it turning the corner, but between herself and the bus there was a narrow street. She halted on the edge of the pavement, gave a hasty glance to right and left, and seeing no traffic, plunged—to collide violently with a man crossing from the other side. As his arms steadied her, she looked up—it seemed a very long way—and found herself staring at Oliver Hobart.

'Oh . . . Oliver!'

'Correct. Madame Brisson, I presume. Trying to break a speed record?'

'My bus.' She made a movement and then stopped. 'Gone.'

'You've forgotten the proverb David taught us: "It isn't enough to hurry; you must start in time." You'll have to use my car.'

In this exchange, brief as it was, she recognised most of the characteristics she remembered from the past. No excited

89

exclamation, like hers. No fancy-seeing-you-here. He had never wasted words or emotion; while others fussed, he calmly went about straightening out the situation.

It was not surprising that he was so tall—at fourteen, he had overtopped David Selby, who had not been a small man—but she had not expected him to be so broad. He had widened. He had been tall and slim, but now he would be described as a very large man indeed.

Of all the holiday children, she was the one he had taken the most time in getting to know. He had found her easy to torment—she could fly into sudden rages, spit-and-scratch like a cat's, and as soon over. Then he had discovered that she, like himself, had a deep fund of humour, and the tension between them had eased.

'How does it feel to be back?' he asked.

'It's nice,' she said inadequately.

He turned her in the direction from which she had come, and they walked together towards the car park.

'Roberta didn't tell me she'd sent that telegram until it had gone,' he said. 'D'you find her changed?'

'Only to look at. The rest is the same. She'll be surprised to see you. She wasn't expecting you.'

'I know. I wasn't expecting to be here. But Austin got back from Portugal last night and we decided to come down—we've got business in Rocksea.'

'Yours, or his?'

'His, but it's my business to keep an eye on his business. I suppose Roberta's told you that he's giving away large sums to orphans and refugees?'

'Yes.'

'He keeps it as quiet as things like that can be kept quiet. He has a lot of trouble with his relations.'

'I can imagine. What orphans or refugees can he find in Hine or Rocksea?'

'He's down here to build another apartment block—to his own design. He owns a lot of land round here—he bought when the place was beginning to expand. I would have bought too, if I'd had any money. Land values have shot up.'

'That's not giving money away—that's making it.'

'He's only giving away what he inherited. But like his father and grandfather and their father and grandfather, he's of hard-headed Yorkshire stock and he's got a sound business head. So he's making money as well as giving it away. He's not making excessive profits on his land—he's using it to ward off speculators. What have you been doing in Hine?'

They had reached the car park and he was opening the door of a dark green car.

'I came in to give back a hired car,' she said as she got in. 'Roberta said it was silly to go on paying for it when I could use hers.'

'Did you try using hers before agreeing?'

'No. It looks old, but she says it goes.'

'It goes very well, with six strong men pushing. She forgets little details like oiling and greasing. How are the three of you going to get on in the cottage?'

'Very well, I think. I've taken over the housekeeping.'

'In other words, you've embarked on a slum-clearance job. Elva's a few degrees tidier than Roberta, but that's all. She won't be joining you for some time, will she? I saw her picture in a group in one of the newspapers, taken before they went to South America.'

'She wasn't going. She was only seeing people off. She and Roberta are going to look after upstairs, and I'm going to look after downstairs.'

'Well, you've had a lot of experience in running a house.'

'Not so much. Paul's aunts—great-aunts—ran the house in Quebec. It belonged to them. Paul had lived with them since his parents died, and he thought it would be sensible to go on living there after we were married, because they could keep house while he and I were away on hunting trips. The only real housekeeping I've ever done was when I was looking after my father.'

'Will you go back to Canada?'

'No. Everything went wrong there—my

father's business, his health, my marriage. I want to—'

'—leave it all behind. Any definite plans in view?'

'No. An idea that I might persuade an aunt in France to let me go shares in her nursery school. Nothing else. I was halfway through my training to be a teacher, but I had to give it up, so I've got no qualifications, and not much talent for anything but cooking. It's a pity I'm not gifted, like Roberta. Have you seen the tile designs she's working on?'

'Yes. She's a good artist. A good all-rounder. Did she mention the crab, Sideways?'

'She says she isn't going to do any more.'

'And means it.'

'She wants to paint.'

'That wasn't why she refused to go on with Sideways. Her reason was that she'd got interested in book-binding. Before Sideways, it was mosaics—she did about a dozen very good ones, and sold them to her friends at whacking prices. Now she's busy on tile designs. Would you have come here if she hadn't suggested it?'

'No. Her telegram was a . . . a sort of lifeline.' She paused and looked at the road along which they were driving. 'This isn't the way to Rocksea.'

'We're doing a detour.'

'Why?'

'To go to the kennels—they're only another couple of miles farther on. When I knew you were going to be at the cottage, I decided to get Duke out.'

'Duke?'

'My mother's dog. He's only a year old; he was a present to her from David. I couldn't keep him in London because he's a big dog and I live in small rooms. I would have got him out before, but I didn't want to leave him with Roberta or Elva. They would have liked to have him, but they would have forgotten regular servicing, as for cars. They're both nice girls, but I don't trust them when they're in the grip of whatever it is they're engaged on. Will you mind taking care of Duke?'

'I'll enjoy it. I miss our dogs. So do the twins. Is Duke safe with children?'

'He's better than safe. He's a first-class guard.'

The delight of the dog on being released brought a feeling of tightness to her throat. As she stood listening to his ecstatic barking and watched him leaping, rolling over, leaping again to lick Oliver's hands or cheeks, she wondered how Oliver could have borne to go away and leave him. He was a Labrador, his condition a testimonial to the excellence of the kennels. He leapt into the car before they reached it, settled himself at the back and travelled with his chin resting on Oliver's shoulder.

'Leaving him after visits must have been hard,' she commented.

94

'More than hard. I used to see his eyes all night—and hear his howls.'

He slowed down when he reached the outskirts of Rocksea.

'What do you think of it?' he asked. 'Would you rather have had another Hine, with petrol stations as the principal eye-catchers, and the usual line of shops with people milling about on narrow pavements in front of them?'

'No. But I can understand how some people feel about it.'

'The traditionalists? What amazed me was the fact that there was so much planning interest among the people who lived here. There weren't many of them—the promontory people, the cottagers and the farmers—and I wouldn't have said they would have cared how Rocksea developed. But they did. Caring wouldn't have been much use if Austin hadn't bought land to prevent it getting into the wrong hands—by which I mean the sky-scraper brotherhood. Even today you'd be amazed at the number of people trying to get here to put up multilevel residential blocks, chain stores— the usual marks of progress.'

'Austin's is a residential block.'

'Yes, but low-slung and designed to fit into the background. Wait and see. Or come and visit us from wherever you are, and see.'

They were coming to the sea-facing houses. Parson's House was in sight, and she wished she could express adequately what was in her

95

mind, but her words came out haltingly.

'Oliver, I'm sorry about David and your mother.'

He said nothing for a few moments. Turning on to the promontory road, he glanced at her.

'That's all right,' he said. 'I know.'

'Won't Duke . . . won't he want to be up at Parson's House?'

'No. He understands.' He leaned his head for a moment against the dog's. 'Don't you, Duke?'

Duke indicated that he did, but his mind appeared to be elsewhere. He was sitting bolt upright, his gaze fixed eagerly on the road ahead. For some time, as they drove past the first house, Boulders, it seemed that he was staring at nothing—and then from the gate of the second house in the row—Vistamar— emerged the figure of a very large, elderly woman holding three Great Danes on leashes. Oliver slowed the car.

'Remember her?' he asked.

'Of course. Boris. I would have gone to see her, but Roberta said she was in London. She looks exactly the same as she did when I went away.'

'Yes. Ageless and changeless.'

The three dogs had caught sight of Duke and were straining at the leashes, causing their owner to break into a trot. Oliver stopped the car, and he and Jeanne got out. Duke bounded after them and the four dogs broke into frantic barking to express their pleasure at seeing one another again. Their owner made herself heard over the din—no effort, as her voice was in keeping with her Wagnerian appearance.

'Isn't it lovely to see them all together again? My *dear* Oliver. And . . . surely not little Jeanne? Dear, *dear* girl! Let me look at you. I expect you've forgotten me.'

'No, Lady Cressing,' Jeanne said, and thought that Boris would be very hard to forget.

She had come to live at Rocksea the year Lorna Hobart married David Selby—but it had not been her first appearance in the town. Her father had bought Vistamar many years before as a holiday house for his innumerable children, and Lady Cressing, the youngest of the brood, had first come in the arms of a Nanny, wearing a woolly cap of the kind that she had worn ever since. The family had in those days arrived with a formidable retinue; stores were fetched by the chauffeur from Exeter, and no notice was taken of the modest wares on sale in Rocksea.

The baby in the woolly cap had in time become an overgrown Miss noted for the speed and dash with which she rode hired horses along the paths of Rockcommon. Then war came, and while it continued, Vistamar remained closed and shuttered.

When war ended, the house was once more occupied by various members of the family.

Their visits would have provided observers in Rocksea, had there been any, with an illustrated history of the rapid changes in the social scene. The chauffeur and the car vanished, to be replaced by bicycles. The number of maids dwindled until domestic help had to be sought locally. The well-pressed suits or skirts of the children gave way to faded blue jeans, neat footwear to scruffed sneakers. At last, the family came without attendants, and relied on local shops and local help.

Lady Cressing did not reappear until she came, widow of a baronet, and announced that she had bought Vistamar from her brothers and sisters and was going to occupy it permanently. With her came the last survivor of a once-numerous staff: an aged maid named, appropriately, Trotter.

Nobody knew Trotter's exact age. She was believed to be nearing eighty, but the weight of years did not prevent her from imposing a rule of terror on the local tradespeople. She scrutinised all bills, and at the end of each month marched along the overhead bridge into the town to make shrill protests about overcharging or inaccuracies. She also admonished Lady Cressing when she felt it necessary. There was sometimes serious disagreement between the two, but Trotter always had the last word.

After the initial shock caused by her bulk and her booming, Lorna and David Selby had taken Lady Cressing to their hearts. As Vistamar had no direct access to the beach, they had for years allowed her to take her dogs through their garden. This privilege—like Lorna's occupation of Parson's House—had been abruptly terminated by Maurice Selby immediately after his brother's death.

Despite the changes in social levels, the inhabitants of Rocksea discovered that to Lady Cressing, things were as they had been in her youth. Attempts to cut her down to size, to make her understand that she was now just like everybody else, fell flat. She ignored the order of precedence in shops, issued peremptory commands and appointed herself a one-woman mission for keeping the town up to scratch. She found her way, nobody could explain how, on to every committee of note, and once on, elected herself to the Chair.

Rocksea, failing to defeat or deflate her, ending by according her the post of town eccentric. But eccentric, or crazy, or simply an anachronism, she was accorded respect.

To Jeanne, she brought back the past as nothing had yet done. Nothing about her seemed changed—grey hair under a home-knitted woollen cap, trousers tucked into short boots, a coat reaching to her thighs. To the holiday children, she had looked a Russian figure, and they had given her the name Boris.

'My dear child!' She had got the dogs under control. 'You take me back so many, many years! Divorced, Oliver told me, and a good thing too if there was no hope of making the thing work, so *useless* to flog a dead horse. I wish it had been as easy in my day, but one had to go on putting up with the wretched creatures however impossible they became. How lovely to see Duke again! My dogs missed him dreadfully. You've heard, I suppose, Jeanne, that I now have to go miles round the long way in order to get them down to the beach? Never, Oliver, never as long as I live will I forgive that man, not only on my account, but also on your dear mother's. I can't *tell* you how I miss her! I don't exaggerate when I say that a light has gone out. I feel as though I'm living in a social, not to say intellectual desert nowadays, left with no neighbours except yourself, so seldom here, and poor decrepit old Mrs Datchet, too deaf to communicate, and the Ugandans, who shut themselves up in Boulders. Have you been to their shop yet, Jeanne?'

'Yes. Roberta took me.'

'Such charmers, those two young people, and so good about bringing me little gifts of spices, so useful if only I could wean Trotter from boiled chicken. What would I have done without Suni to exercise my dogs when I'm away? Now you mustn't keep me chatting, or these dogs will go mad. Would you like me to add Duke to the string?'

'If you'd be so—' began Oliver.

'Oh, no trouble, no trouble at all, a pleasure. The only irritating thing is not being able to slip down through the garden of Parson's House as I used to. Oliver, dear boy, if you're staying any length of time, you'll notice that you now get your letters an hour earlier. It was *too* much, having to wait for one's mail while that lecherous old postman dawdled along making love to all the housewives on the way. I let Curzon bite him, not a big bite, just a little one, and there were the usual complaints and fuss, but I noticed when I got back yesterday from London that we now have a very spritely young man who arrives in time for me to read my post before luncheon, such a difference to one's day. Jeanne, my dear, if you and the other girls in the cottage have any trouble over milk supplies, you must let me know at once. There is no shortage whatsoever; it's simply the milkman's way of blackmailing his customers into buying those extras he wants to sell. I don't have any difficulty because he leaves his van outside my house while he goes down to the last three houses, and all I have to do is slip out and help myself, and nobody the wiser, and if I remember, I put the money into the poor box on Sundays. So you must let me know if you can't get as much milk as you need for those children of yours—twins, I hear, identical, charming, charming. Now we've all chatted enough. I'm not going to say a word about what's going on at Parson's House, because if ever a man deserved to run into trouble, it's Maurice Selby, and I hope the next lot of workmen fall downstairs too, though I'm so sorry for poor Mr Quinter, such a nice man, and so anxious to do well in Rocksea. Goodbye for now. I shall be very offended if you young people don't drop in on me now and then. I won't offer you a cooked meal, because poor old Trotter really is past it, but I can supply any liquid refreshment from lemon squash to vodka, and one of my brothers has just sent me some delicious olives as large as apricots, so we shall share them when you come. Goodbye, goodbye. Come along, Duke; we'll be glad to have you. He'll find his own way back to you, I daresay, Oliver. And before I go, may I ask if you really meant what you said when you gave me permission to go down to the beach through the cottage garden?'

'Whenever you like,' Oliver said.

'That's very kind. Jeanne, my dear, you need not have the slightest uneasiness about the dogs frightening the children. I won't go that way now, in case they get alarmed, but you must tell them that the dogs love them, and they never, never bite without my permission. One thing I can say about my animals; they're all *gentlemen*.'

She walked down the road and turned seaward. Jeanne drew a deep breath.

'She made me feel fourteen years old,' she said, getting into the car.

'She's indestructible,' Oliver said. 'What was that she said about Parson's House?'

'She said that Maurice Selby had run into trouble.'

'What sort of trouble? Something connected with the house?'

Jeanne hesitated.

'It's a long story,' she said at last. 'Wait till we're having lunch.'

He drove to the cottage and stopped the car outside the kitchen door. It was open, and they could see Austin at the table cutting bread and passing the slices over to Roberta to be buttered. At the sight of Jeanne, he gave a loud cry of welcome, dropped the loaf and came to meet her.

'This is the moment I've waited for all these long and dreary intervening years,' he told her, taking her into a warm embrace. 'You haven't changed in any particular, and it doesn't seem to me that you've even grown. I can't describe my feelings at having you back with us, because as you can see, when my deepest emotions are stirred, I'm tongue-tied.'

'Like Boris,' Oliver commented, brushing past with his suitcase.

'You met her?' Roberta asked.

'Just outside her gate. She took Duke along.'

'Duke? You got him out of the kennels? Good. If you're hungry, there'll be food in a minute. We had to come up and get some because Austin emptied the picnic basket.

Where did you meet Jeanne?'

'In Hine. She butted me in the stomach.' He had opened his suitcase and was unloading provisions. The twins came from the bedroom and stood still to stare at yet another stranger. Oliver glanced down at them.

'Hello,' he said.

There was no response.

'They don't talk for the first hour or so,' Roberta explained. 'They just stand drinking you in.'

'Names?'

'Polly and Jo, but it doesn't matter much, because they both come when you call.'

'If you come here and look inside this suitcase,' Oliver told them, 'you might see something you like. But you have to say Hello first.'

'Hello,' they said simultaneously.

'That's it. Now come and look.'

They came and peered anxiously. From the case, Oliver drew out two long cardboard boxes.

'Boats,' he told them. 'One's a schooner and the other's a barge. Jo—whichever Jo is—can have the barge today, and Polly can have the schooner. Tomorrow, you change over. Like them?'

'Yes.'

'What else?'

'Thank you very much.'

'Fine. Off you go.'

104

Austin, opening a bottle of wine, was muttering to himself.

'Currying favour. Comes in loaded with gifts, like Lord Bountiful. A bad sign; shows he can't rely on his charm, like the rest of us can.' He raised his voice and spoke protestingly. 'Jeanne, you've only laid three places—where's Oliver going to sit?'

'You've had your lunch,' Jeanne told him. 'And the twins' lunch too.'

He pulled another chair to the table.

'Nobody's going to starve me,' he said firmly, 'just because I pecked at a sandwich or two on the beach.'

Oliver, going upstairs with his suitcase, came down again in jeans and a sports shirt. They sat round the table, while the twins went into the bathroom and filled the bath with water in order to sail their vessels.

'To more reunions.' Austin raised his glass. 'Pity Elva isn't here. In a way, it's a pity Paul isn't here too—Jeanne, did you get those fat letters of his? I put them on . . . Yes, you've got them. If you're thinking of answering them, you can tell him we're grateful to him for giving you back to us. It's almost like Parson's House all over again.'

'Speaking of Parson's House,' Oliver said, 'they don't seem to have got far with the work on it. From my window, I couldn't see a single workman on the place.'

'And there won't be,' Roberta said.

105

'Why not?'

'There's a hitch.'

'New name for a strike?' Austin asked.

'No. There's a hold-up.'

'Who's doing the holding-up?' Oliver asked.

'That,' Roberta answered, 'nobody knows. Rumours are rife, whatever rife means. Jeanne and I first heard them when I took her to the Spice Box the day after she arrived. Suni mentioned them, but his grandfather stopped him from telling us what they were. Then Mr Quinter came to see us, and he gave us the whole story.'

'Quinter? The builder who's doing the job?' Oliver asked.

'The builder who was doing the job, past tense. First the men went, then his partner went, then the scaffolding went and then the board in front of the house went. But when he came to see us, he was still on the job. We went up to the house and—'

'You went up to Parson's House?' Oliver broke in.

'Yes.'

'Inside?'

'Yes. There are rumours,' she said, 'that the house is haunted.'

There was a long silence.

'Haunted?' It was Austin's voice. 'Parson's House—haunted?'

'That's right. Haunted,' Roberta said.

'Is this supposed to be a joke?' Oliver asked.

106

'No. No joke. A black joke, maybe—but serious for Mr Quinter. He—'

'Suppose you give us the whole story?' Oliver suggested.

'I can only tell you as much as we know of it. Rumours went round the town that there was a lot of funny business going on at the house, and the workmen were getting scared and leaving. The point is that nobody knows whether the rumours started first, or the ... the manifestations.'

'What manifestations, for God's sake?' Oliver asked impatiently.

'Nobody's actually *seen* anything. But the workmen—and old Mrs Clermont too—felt when they were inside the house that something or someone was close to them, touching them. Mr Quinter's men were getting scared, and leaving, so he went to see Maurice Selby in London, and he was told that if he couldn't get men to work, there were other builders who could. He was given a week to get his men back on the job.'

'What was his idea in coming to see you?'

'His wife remembered that we'd lived there once, and he came to ask if there'd been any funny business in our time. Jeanne and I went up to the house with him and walked through it, so's he could tell people there was nothing there.'

'I see. And having walked through the house, what was your report?'

107

'Nothing there. The only trouble was that just as Mr Quinter was going away, we heard—'

'A man fell off a ladder,' Jeanne broke in. 'Mr Quinter's partner.'

'Extraordinary.' Oliver's voice was cold. 'And did Mrs Clermont fall off a ladder too?'

'No. She fell downstairs,' Roberta answered. 'Something frightened her.'

'What frightened the chap on the ladder?' Austin asked.

'He said the window just above him, which had been closed, opened suddenly and swept him off.'

There was a pause.

'Perhaps I've got it wrong,' Oliver said at last. 'Did I hear you say that you two ostensibly sane women agreed to go up to—'

'It wasn't a bad idea,' Austin interrupted. 'If there'd been anything up there, Roberta would have found it. Remember her London friend? Is this why all those people have been standing outside the house goggling?'

'Yes. Mr Quinter's partner,' Jeanne said, 'had a theory about the rumours. He said he believed that someone was trying to get their revenge on Maurice Selby for something he'd done to them.'

'Revenge?' Austin spoke thoughtfully. 'I can understand there might be people who'd like to hurt him—but not this way. Any possibility that Quinter himself could have had something

108

to do with it? It must have brought him a good deal of publicity.'

'No,' Jeanne said. 'Not Mr Quinter. He was worried sick.'

'I don't suppose he staged his partner's fall off the ladder,' Oliver said. 'If it's an attempt to make trouble for Maurice Selby, why not make real trouble, instead of merely spreading rumours about ghosts?'

'What better way could anybody get at him,' Austin pointed out, 'than by making his house a target for sensation-seekers? Think back to that row he had with David when David married your mother. What upset him most was the thought of leaving the house. He wouldn't sell it to David because he thought, or hoped the marriage wouldn't last, and he could come back to the house again. He turned your mother out and now he's got the house— and just as he's about to take possession, this ghost thing comes up and the work comes to a stop. He can't be very happy about it, especially as he's sold his house in London. So spreading ghost rumours isn't as silly as it sounds. At the same time—'

He was brought up by an exclamation from Jeanne. Following her glance, the others saw a wide, swiftly-flowing river entering the kitchen from the hall. When they stood up, they found themselves wading. Through the open door of the bathroom they saw the twins, oblivious to anything but their boats, launching them from the overflowing bath on to the pool on the bathroom floor.

'Polly! Jo! Look what—'

Austin's voice broke into her exclamations.

'Calm, if you please. Everybody calm. Keep your cools. Leave this to me—I'm dressed for it.'

Barefoot, he went with crane-like steps into the bathroom and turned off the taps. The twins were following their boats into the hall.

'Hey, wait for me,' he called.

He carried out the bathroom stool and placed it upside down in the middle of the stream.

'Now *this* way,' he said, 'we can have two-way traffic. Push the barge over here, Polly-Jo. That's right.'

Oliver eyed the flood. When he spoke, he sounded more irritable than he felt—but the incident had interrupted his lunch, and he was still hungry.

'The patter of little feet,' he commented.

Jeanne swung round to face him, and he found himself witness to one of the flashes of rage which in the past had scorched him when he drove her too far. Her cheeks were flushed, her eyes dark with anger.

'They won't worry you,' she snapped. 'You live upstairs.'

'I can hardly stay upstairs indefinitely, can I?' he asked coldly. 'This is, after all, my house.'

110

'No, it is not! For now, *not*.' Her English was slipping. 'You have rented it to us, so it is ours, and if you don't like my children you can go and stay where Austin is staying, and then you won't be troubled.'

'I certainly won't be troubled,' he said. 'I'll see to that.'

'You brought the boats. It was your fault.'

Roberta, an interested onlooker, spoke.

'I'll second that,' she said. 'His fault entirely.'

CHAPTER FOUR

The next day, Jeanne and the twins were early on the beach. There had been only their own picnic to prepare, and few preparations for dinner, since she knew nothing of any plans the others might have made for the day.

All but Jeanne had dined out the night before. She had made the twins her excuse for not going with them. They had returned late; Austin had returned with them and they had made coffee in the kitchen, closing the doors and keeping their voices low in order not to disturb the sleepers. But this morning, lying on the sand, idly scooping up handfuls and letting them fall through her fingers, Jeanne realised that the peaceful interlude was over. Austin might sleep in his room at the hotel, and he and Oliver had work to do and would presumably be out all day, but for the rest of the time, the cottage would be the meeting place for them all.

She saw Oliver coming down the steps, Duke at his heels. He walked past her to where the twins were playing, picked them up, carried one under each arm to the water and launched them. He followed them, adapting his stroke to their dog-paddle, and finding them unafraid to submerge, played games in which Duke joined. Finally they came out of the water, breathless and dripping. The twins wrapped their towels round them and Oliver dropped on to the sand beside Jeanne.

'Good morning. Nice children,' he remarked. 'A bit small for their age?'

'They are just the right size.'

'If you say so.'

'They've grown since they left Canada. I notice it in clothes. I shall have to prolong their dresses.'

'Lengthen.'

'Lengthen?'

'You don't prolong dresses.'

'But to prolong is to make longer.'

'Not dresses. Though of course if you lengthen them, you prolong their period of usefulness.'

'But—'

'You're not going to tell me that I can't speak my own language?'

'No. But when we were young, you used to tell me things that were wrong, to confuse me.'

'Not to confuse you. To demonstrate some of the difficulties foreigners encounter, so that you could avoid them.'

'Then I shall lengthen the children's dresses. So they can't be too small, as you said.'

'It's a pity you deprived them of a father.'

He was rubbing his towel over his hair, his face hidden, but she knew that if she could see it, it would be wearing the bland expression that accompanied his more provocative remarks.

'I didn't deprive them of a father,' she said evenly. 'In the way you're thinking of it, they didn't have a father.'

His face emerged from the towel, and he subjected her to a long, frank survey.

'What went wrong, exactly?' he asked. 'I've heard Roberta's version; I'd like to hear yours.'

'Nothing went wrong. Everything went as it had to go. The only mistake was in thinking that Paul could stop hunting and—'

'—hurry home from the office in time to put the children to bed. Odd how we all knew him better than you did. We—'

'—could have warned me. I know. Roberta said so. It's a pity I didn't write to ask your advice before I married him.'

'Offended?'

'No. Only tired of being told I shouldn't have married him.' She paused, her eyes

113

unseeingly on the two dinghies setting out from a neighbouring beach. 'Sometimes I think my father would have said so too, if things had been different. But he was ill, very ill, and there wasn't much money, and Paul was an old friend of mine and it must have been nice for my father to think, or to make himself believe that I was going to be looked after when he died.'

'Do you remember our discussions about what we were all going to be when we grew up?'

'Yes. You were going to be a surgeon, like your father. How did you turn into an accountant?'

'By deciding that I'd like to work with figures.'

'But that is not so interesting.'

'Figures aren't dull. They're complicated. Challenging. Rows and rows, columns and columns that would mean nothing to a layman, but which an expert can handle as a general handles armies. Very satisfying. Now I come to think of it, most of the accountants I know are very relaxed men. They know what they're dealing with. No psychological problems. You were going to be a nurse. What made you switch to teaching?'

Her only answer was a shrug. The children brought her some shells and she gave them her attention until they returned to their sand castle. Then she turned to Oliver.

114

'Is it really true that your mother was told to leave Parson's House? I mean to say, was it really done in . . . in such an insulting way?'

'Insulting, no. Unfeeling, yes. She was going anyway; she had no intention of stopping in a house that wasn't hers, a house that belonged to a man who disliked her.'

'Apart from how it was done, did she mind leaving the house?'

He paused before answering.

'Strangely enough, no,' he said at last. 'If it had been David's, and David could have left it to her so that she could have left it to me, she would have been pleased, but she knew from the first that their tenancy depended on Maurice. When he married a year or so ago, they wrote and offered him Parson's House, but he refused because his wife didn't want to leave London. But my mother always, so to speak, had a suitcase packed and ready to pick up.'

'Roberta said she got ill because—'

'Not because she had to leave the house. She wasn't well for some time before David died. Losing him and losing the house so soon afterwards made her very depressed. How well do you remember her?'

'Oh, perfectly! It's true, isn't it, that we all— all the holiday children—loved her?'

'Yes, I think it is.'

'She and David made us so happy . . .'

'It wasn't all on one side. They both looked

115

forward to the day he'd have to take the pony and trap into Exeter to meet whichever of you had arrived. And they did a good deal of preparation before the holidays. David used to remove the rugs and put the second-best covers on the sofas and chairs, and put away anything that children might damage. They turned it into a place for children. Did Paul ever talk about Parson's House?'

'Only about your mother. He often talked about her. I think, although she didn't show it, that he was her favourite.'

'Wrong. I was. I'm glad you remember her.'

'The first night I came here, Roberta said that when there's a moon and the light shines on the terrace where your mother and David used to sit, she can see your mother's white dress—and she asked me if I could see it, but I couldn't, and in a way I was sorry. I don't believe in ghosts the way she does, but all the same, if you love someone, and they die, perhaps to see their ghost would make you feel they were near you. Do you feel that?'

'No. If you've got memories, why do you need ghosts?'

They fell silent, and when he spoke again, it was on a different subject.

'I forgot to tell you—Elva rang up. I took the call just before coming down. She's arriving at Exeter at five-twenty. I suppose you'd like to go and meet her?'

'Yes, I would.'

'I can't take you there. Neither can Austin—we're both going to be busy from three to five. You could take Roberta with you for identification purposes, but you won't need her. What Elva was, Elva is, except for a few minor adjustments. You won't find her very companionable—she's pretty self-contained. But she's got a lot of sense and she doesn't talk as much as Roberta does. She hasn't had much of a life, one way and another.'

'It was all right when her mother was alive, wasn't it?'

'Not really. Her mother's interest was centred on her husband. Being left out didn't seem to have much effect on Elva; she decided to behave as though she had no parents, which I suppose was the best way of meeting the situation.' He paused. 'We were talking about ghosts. I had an idea last night—I thought I'd go and see Quinter.'

'To talk about the rumours?'

'No. To ask him for the key of the house. I'd like to take a last look round, and this'll be my last chance to get in. If Maurice Selby's anywhere around, of course I won't want to go in, but Quinter'll know where he is. Did we disturb you when we came in last night?'

'No.'

'Why didn't you come? It would have been perfectly easy to arrange a twin-sitter.'

'I wanted to stay with them. I mean at night. Everything is strange for them.' She hesitated.

'And it isn't only the children. It's me, too.' She turned to him, and he saw tears in her eyes. 'Do you know how happy I am now? Happy for the first time for . . . for years, I think. I'm happy to be here, happy to be in a place I know and like, happy to be doing something I like doing, something I can do well. How I feel is . . . I don't know how to express it . . . I feel that I want to enjoy these things as they come, waking up every morning thinking how wonderful life is, after all. For now, the children and myself and the cottage are enough; I don't want anything else. I don't want to go out to meet strangers—not yet.'

'My mother knew you very well. She said you were a very small squirrel, collecting and storing against future shortages. Don't tie yourself up too tightly to the twins. You may tell yourself that it's just for the moment, but it could become a habit. Next time we dine out, come with us.'

'I might. But mostly, I feel I can make better food, or just as good food, at home.'

Austin, coming down in time to hear these last remarks, pointed out that the food was not the whole pleasure in dining out.

'The company, too,' he said. 'And the wine and the music, if there's music. What happened to all those play-gypsy-play chaps that used to bend tenderly over our mothers as they supped their soup?'

Jeanne scarcely heard him; she was staring

118

in amazement at his beach robe. He was wearing a pale pink jacket made of towelling. It reached halfway down his thighs, leaving his long, stick-like legs bare.

'You like my outfit?' he asked her.

'Well . . . no.'

'That's because you haven't seen it all.' He opened the jacket to display purple towelling trunks. 'These went with the jacket. I was asked to swim in Lisbon, and had nothing to swim in, so I found a shop and the shop found the latest in twin suitings.' He settled himself beside her on the sand. 'We missed you last night.'

'Where did you dine?'

'At Cristall's—where could you get better food? It's a pity you weren't there. Mr Cristall stood us brandy with our coffee, and regaled us with all the latest scandal. And there was an unattached man you might have found interesting.'

'Too old,' Oliver said.

'Well, yes,' Austin admitted. 'But he was good-looking in his way, and he looked well-turned-out, the sort that make women think of them as good escorts. Where's Roberta?'

'Don't know,' Oliver said. 'But if it's company you want, here comes Boris.'

Duke had already gone to meet her. The twins, looking up in the act of shaping the battlements of a fort, caught sight of the majestic figure coming down in the wake of three enormous dogs, and remained open-mouthed. Jeanne wondered whether this first sight of Lady Cressing would be a landmark in their memories.

Her voice seemed to fill the little beach.

'Good morning, good morning! What a magnificent day! I do hope you won't mind my joining you. Where shall I sit?'

The twins watched her select the spot. Then they watched, fascinated, as she unrolled a large towel and spread it on the sand. Next, she opened a large golf umbrella and propped it against a rock. From a voluminous bag she took two books and a writing pad, another towel as big as a sheet, and a Thermos flask. This last she held up before the twins.

'Nice cool water for my dogs,' she told them. 'You don't need to bring any for Duke, because if he gets thirsty, all he has to do is go up the steps to his bowl of water outside the cottage. But my dogs can't get at theirs, so I bring some for them. Now I think, before going in to swim, I'll do a little sunbathing.'

From the bag came a bottle of sun-tan lotion. Divesting herself of her long beach robe, she revealed limbs that were massive, but still firm and surprisingly shapely. She applied a generous layer of lotion, replaced the bottle in the bag and lowered herself on to her towel.

'Lovely.' She gave a sigh of pleasure. 'Simply *lovely*. Aren't we lucky to have this beautiful beach to ourselves? Aren't we fortunate to live

120

in this lovely spot? Do you know, whenever my husband and I disagreed, I used to recall my young days and I used to say to myself "I wish I were back in Rocksea". I thought that if ever he died, which seemed too much to hope for, I would come straight back here. Which I did. It meant making rather complicated financial adjustments with all my brothers and sisters, and as they're extremely difficult to deal with, that took some time, but I managed it in the end and here I am. I hope, Jeanne, dear, that you're as happy to be back as I am.'

'Can't you persuade her to stop here?' Austin asked. 'She's merely touching down before taking off again for France.'

'You must leave her to make her own decisions. But she mustn't run away too soon; she needs time in which to rest and make plans for the future. All the same, I can't think of any place in which she and the twins would be healthier and happier than here. Austin, dear boy, forgive me; I speak as an old friend: do you really think that costume suits you?'

'It looked better in the shop,' he confessed. 'You know how it is? You buy a straw hat in Italy and it looks just like everybody else's, and then you put it on in England and you stop the traffic.'

'Perhaps it's the colours,' Lady Cressing said, her eyes still on the purple and pink. 'As a nation, we don't go in much for rainbow hues. It seems almost out of character for us to have such a brightly-coloured national flag. Now I must stop chatting and have my dip.'

She held out two well-shaped white hands, and Oliver and Austin sprang to their feet to raise her gently to hers. She put on a black bathing cap and strode purposefully to the water. With her went the four dogs, and behind the dogs went the twins, determined not to lose any of this entertainment. All eyes were on her as she splashed through the shallow water, paused when it was at waist level and then with a sweep of her arms launched herself on to a wave and swam in a slow breast stroke for a few hundred yards, then turned and swam back again.

'And that's all,' she said, taking the towel which Austin held ready, and enveloping herself in it. 'Brief, but beneficial.' She took off her cap, shook out her short, grey-wool hair and lay back on her outspread robe. 'And now I shall send Curzon to fetch my luncheon basket. Curzon, go on, there's a good fellow.'

Curzon bounded away. The eyes of the twins opened so widely that Lady Cressing offered an explanation.

'I don't care for sandwiches,' she told them, 'and I only eat a light dinner, so I like something substantial in the middle of the day. So my maid, who is called Trotter, prepares a meal and she puts it into little dishes which have a lower compartment for hot water to keep the food warm, just like the bowls you probably had your porridge in when you were smaller. Trotter puts the dishes into a basket and straps the basket on to Curzon's back, and he brings it to me. As you know, dogs are very intelligent animals and they understand almost at once what it is you want them to do. Isn't that Roberta coming down? And surely that's Mr Quinter with her?'

'I was going to pay him a visit,' Oliver said. 'He's saved me the journey.'

Roberta was wearing almost nothing. Mr Quinter was in a warm-looking suit, his only concession to the heat being a new soft straw hat too large for him. Oliver spread a towel for him on the sand and he sat down, his expression strained in the effort to avoid looking at the areas of bare flesh so freely displayed by the three ladies.

'Thanks, Mr Hobart,' he muttered in acknowledgment of the towel. 'Morning, m'lady, 'Mornin' all.' He jerked his head in the direction of Parson's House. 'I suppose you all know that I've been taken off the job?'

'Yes. Anybody else taking over?' Oliver asked.

Mr Quinter nodded.

'Firm from Exeter. I'm not worried much. This little affair hasn't done me as much 'arm as I thought. A lot of people are saying I couldn't 'ave been expected to work with all this spook business goin' on.'

'I was coming up to see you,' Oliver said. 'I

wondered whether you'd stretch a point and let me have the key to the house. Mr Selby certainly wouldn't let me in—we're not friends—so this is my last chance.'

'He's got no friends that I've 'eard of,' Mr Quinter said. 'If you want to go in, it'd 'ave to be this morning, because I'm goin' in later on to hand over the keys to 'is office in Exeter.'

'Is Mr Selby there?'

'Not that I know. Last I 'eard, 'e was in London and so was Mrs Selby.' He hesitated. 'You ever met 'er, sir?'

'No.'

'Well, I did, when I went to London to talk to Mr Selby. And what stuck out a mile, because she didn't care who knew it, was that she didn't want to come and live in Rocksea. And that's why I came along to see you this morning. I've been thinking, and what I thought was this: suppose it was Mrs Selby who started the ghost rumours? Once the talk started, it wouldn't matter whether the men on the job get the jitters or whether they didn't; all she'd 'ave to tell Mr Selby was that she wouldn't come and live in a 'aunted 'ouse.'

'She could hardly have started the rumours from London,' Lady Cressing objected.

'I don't know how she'd do it, m'lady,' Mr Quinter said stubbornly, 'but she struck me as someone who'd know how to go about fixing things the way she wanted them, and she's someone who'd benefit if people said there

124

were ghosts in the 'ouse. If I was asked to pick out a rumour-starter, I'd pick on her.'

'There's another theory which they were discussing at the hotel this morning,' Austin said. 'The possibility that the parson has come back to haunt the house because Selby turned his daughter—the parson's daughter—out of it.'

'We can put it to the test,' Oliver said lightly. 'If it's my grandfather, I ought to sense his presence. Have you got the keys with you?' he asked Mr Quinter.

'Yes. Mind if I come with you?'

'You can all go, and leave me with the twins,' Lady Cressing said. 'I've no wish to go into the house, thank you. And here comes Curzon with my luncheon.'

The twins sat down to watch her unpack the basket. The others climbed the path to Parson's House. Duke followed them, and Austin remarked that if there was anything supernatural inside the house, the dog would sense it.

'That's true enough,' Mr Quinter said. 'Animals always know.'

But Duke, having reached the front door, sat down and refused to go inside. He showed no sign of uneasiness; he merely indicated that he preferred to wait where he was. Oliver ordered him sharply inside, but Jeanne spoke with her eyes on the dog.

'Don't make him,' she said. 'Let him do

what he wants to do.'

'That's right; let 'im be,' Mr Quinter said. 'I'm going to stay outside with him.'

'Why?' Oliver asked.

'Because I don't believe in ghosts, that's why, and I don't want to 'ave to change my mind. Leave the dog with me and we'll keep an eye on each other.'

They went in without him, and for Austin it proved, as it had done for Jeanne and Roberta, a journey into the past. Their thoughts were not on ghosts; at every turn, in every room, upstairs and down, there were memories: the hook placed almost ceiling-high by Oliver to prevent the less tall Paul from snatching the wrong mackintosh on his way out; the marks on the window-sill of Elva's room, made when she gave a demonstration of sliding down a rope to escape if a fire broke out; the faint traces of arrows that had been drawn one wet day by the hares to guide the hounds.

They ended their tour in the drawing room, and sat on the wide window seat, gazing absently at the dust covers.

'Silly to think of ghosts in this house,' Austin remarked after a time. 'All I've thought of since we came in isn't ghosts, but what we used to do here. Remember that Christmas when we all decided to get dressed up?'

'You were a Chinaman, old style,' Roberta recalled. 'You made a long pigtail out of black wool and wore Lorna's Chinese dressing gown.'

'That's right. And Lorna was a Roman matron, in a sheet. Oliver was in a sheet too, with an Arab headdress.'

'An oil sheik, new style,' Oliver said. 'Why was Paul draped in towels?'

'Ben Hur,' Jeanne said. 'And we all went over to show Boris how we looked.'

'All of which,' Austin observed, 'is a long haul from an unseen presence pushing people downstairs. What did you think of Quinter's theory about Mrs Selby?' he asked Oliver.

'Far-fetched,' Oliver answered. 'There are people nearer home who could have started the rumours. Old Mrs Datchet, for example, who still bears a grudge against Maurice Selby because he sacked her son and refused to give him any references. And how about Suni, who might like to get his own back over that car business?'

'What car business?' Jeanne asked.

'When David died,' Oliver explained, 'Suni wanted to buy his car. My mother agreed to let him have it, but there was difficulty about his finding all the money at once, so she agreed to let him pay by instalments. He paid the first instalment and was about to take over the car, when my mother died, and Maurice claimed the car. He refused to believe there'd been any agreement or any payment, and as Suni unfortunately had nothing in writing, he couldn't stop him from taking the car. So if he heard that Selby was coming to live here, he might have thought of a way of making trouble. I'm just putting it forward as a possibility, but not a likely one; you might just as well pin the thing on Boris, who certainly wasn't pleased at having to take her dogs to the beach the long way round.'

'Seems unwise of Selby to have given the job-finishing to an Exeter firm,' Austin remarked. 'They're bound to hear what happened to Quinter's lot. It would have been better to send down a London firm.'

'A lot more expensive,' Oliver pointed out, and rose. 'Let's give back the keys.'

They went round to make certain that all doors and windows were securely fastened. On the window-sill in the kitchen was a red woollen scarf which Roberta thought might belong to one of the workmen. She suggested taking it out to Mr Quinter.

'No. Leave it,' Oliver said. 'If it's one of his men's, he can come and fetch it, but it looks to me more like the thing Mrs Clermont always has draped round her neck.'

They went out, gave back the keys, thanked Mr Quinter and informed him that they had encountered nothing inside the house but memories. They were not anxious to linger; the realisation that this might be the last time any of them entered the house had sobered them. They walked to the little gate that Maurice Selby had ordered removed. Then Roberta paused.

'Mr Quinter, there was a red scarf on the kitchen window-sill,' she said. 'We left it because we thought it might belong to Mrs Clermont.'

'Knitted scarf?' he asked.

'Yes.'

'Mine,' he said. 'Glad to get it back. My wife knitted it, and she didn't look pleased when I said I didn't know where I'd lost it.'

'I'll go in and get it for you,' Austin offered.

'No, thanks. I'll go, Mr Parkes. If four of you can stay in the house as long as you did, and nothing to show for it, then there's nothing there.' He turned back to the house. 'Shan't be a mo.'

They waited for him, looking down at Lady Cressing and the twins on the beach. When some time had elapsed, Oliver frowned.

'What's he doing?' he asked.

There was no need for anybody to answer. Mr Quinter had come out of the house. He paused a moment to steady himself, and then took a few stumbling steps towards them. Oliver and Austin were beside him in a moment, holding his arms. His face was mottled, his breath coming in gasps.

'What's the matter?' Oliver asked. 'What happened?'

Mr Quinter, unable to speak, shook his head. Then he drew a deep breath and managed to bring out a few hoarse words.

'I'd like to . . . to sit down.'

They helped him to the bench outside the drawing room window, lowered him on to it and stood round anxiously, waiting for him to recover. At last he took out a handkerchief, wiped his damp forehead and looked from one to the other of the watchers.

'My scarf,' he said unsteadily. 'It was mine, all right.'

There was a pause.

'I'll get it,' Austin said.

'No. Wait.' Mr Quinter made an effort to regain his self-command. 'Wait till I tell you what happened.'

They waited.

'I went into the kitchen and I saw the scarf 'anging on the 'ook behind the door. I was walking out with the scarf in my hand, and then . . . then somebody, something pulled it away. Pulled it right out of my 'and. I looked down, thinking maybe the dog 'ad come in and taken it, playing, like. But the dog wasn't there. There was only me. But I swear to you I didn't drop the scarf. It was a kind of quick flick— one moment I 'ad it, the next moment it was on the floor a few feet away. And I don't know 'ow long it was before I could move. And then I left it where it was lying, and got out of the 'ouse, thank God. And that's enough for me. Mr Selby can 'ave his job, and welcome.'

Nobody spoke. Then Oliver walked into the house and a moment later returned with the

130

scarf in his hand. He locked the front door and brought the keys to Mr Quinter.

'Thanks. Thanks a lot, Mr Hobart.'

'How do you feel about driving home?' Oliver asked him. 'I could easily take you back in your car, and walk back.'

'No.' Mr Quinter rose. 'No, thanks. I'm all right, Mr Hobart. Just so long as I don't 'ave to go inside the 'ouse any more, I'll be fine.' He walked to the gate and then paused and turned. 'If you don't mind, I'd rather you didn't mention this turn-up to anybody. Not yet, anyway. I might tell my wife, and then again, I might not. And my last word is that I didn't drop that scarf.'

They heard his car as he drove away. And then into the silence Roberta threw a desperate-sounding sentence.

'There must be something in there!' She swung round to face Oliver. 'There must be, Oliver, there *must* be!'

'Wait a minute.' Austin spoke quietly. 'We don't know it all yet. Where did you find the scarf?' he asked Oliver.

'Where we left it—on the window-sill in the kitchen.'

'He said it was hanging up behind the door. Why would he say that if it was on the window-sill?' Roberta demanded. 'Why?'

'Sit on the bench,' Oliver said, 'and let's try and figure out why.' He waited until she was seated. 'This is a test case. We can come down

131

on one side or the other—an unseen presence in Parson's House—or not. We all saw Mr Quinter go inside. We all saw him come out. Something obviously happened inside the house to reduce him to the state he was in when he came out again. But exactly what was it?'

'I'm asking you,' Roberta said angrily. 'You're supposed to be doing the figuring-out, not me. Mr Quinter's workmen, Mrs Clermont, Mr Quinter's partner and now Mr Quinter himself—are they all liars?'

'No. But the men,' Oliver pointed out, 'started the work under a cloud of rumour, and the first mishap must have made them uneasy. Panic's contagious. Mrs Clermont caught the bug. Falling off a ladder is something that can happen to anybody, any time they climb up one. Mr Quinter, like Mrs Clermont, had the bug, but in his case it didn't become active until he found himself in the house—alone— just now. He was already half-convinced that there was something odd about the house. He was ready to be fully convinced, and he tipped the balance because he's a middle-aged man who is too overweight to stand the kind of heat we've been having this morning, especially in the warm suit he was wearing, and even more especially when he had walked down to the beach and sat trying not to look at Boris's bosom or Roberta's thighs or Jeanne's lovely legs. Each one of us can form an opinion; I'm merely giving you mine. I'm convinced that Mr Quinter was suffering from over-exposure—to rumours, to ghost stories, to anxiety about the job and the humiliation of losing it.' He paused. 'Any questions?'

'Yes.' Roberta got to her feet. 'How fast can we get down to the cottage and have a drink?'

CHAPTER FIVE

Roberta, uncertain throughout the afternoon whether to go with Jeanne and the twins to Exeter to meet Elva, at last decided on another plan: she would stay at home with the twins, give them their bath and their supper, and if the train was late and Jeanne unduly delayed, put them into bed.

'It'll take my mind off Mr Quinter,' she said. 'I still don't believe that seeing bare bodies on the beach could unbalance him. He might be middle-aged, but he's married, isn't he? I'll stay home and be aunt to the twins. You go and meet Elva.'

Going to meet Elva proved less simple than it sounded. Roberta's car refused to start. Jeanne was not at first worried; it was a temperamental car and she had learned by now that it required patient handling. But this time, there was no response to any of the usual persuasions.

Roberta had gone down to the beach with the children. The two men had left the cottage immediately after lunch. Jeanne considered telephoning for a taxi, and then decided to walk to the hotel to see if Oliver or Austin had left a car there; if so, she would borrow it.

She crossed the main road by the overhead bridge—an experience she thought the twins might enjoy—and crossed the square to the road that led to Cristall's Hotel. She admired as she approached it the ornamental wrought-iron gateway and the curving drive flanked by palm trees; these, with the bright sunshine and the flower-lined hotel, gave a semi-tropical look to the entrance.

Neither of the cars was standing outside. She entered the building and found herself in a very large, low-ceilinged hall, the reception desk so discreetly placed behind banks of fern that she had difficulty in locating it. Could she, she asked, be informed whether Mr Hobart's or Mr Parkes' car was in the garage?

They would find out. They would inform her. In the meantime, would she take a seat?

A page conducted her ceremoniously to one; Mr Cristall, she thought, deserved his four stars. Seated on a divan with the current newspapers and magazines on a table by her side, she was informed presently that Mr Hobart had put his car into the garage twenty minutes ago and was now taking tea in the reading room; perhaps she would care to join

134

him?

Conducted to the reading room, she found Oliver dividing his attention between some official-looking papers, and tea with brown bread and butter and mustard-and-cress sandwiches. He rose and expressed more surprise than pleasure at the sight of her.

'Lost the way to the station?' he enquired.

'No. But—'

'Let me guess. Roberta's car didn't want to go all that way.'

'It wouldn't even start. I came here to see if by any chance you or Austin had left a car here.'

'Sit down.'

'There's no time.'

He pressed a bell.

'Did you have tea before you came out?'

'No.'

'Then you may as well have it now.' He ordered it. 'I'm certainly not going to leave mine.'

'You needn't leave it. If you'd let me take your car—'

'No. Not this time. When we've enjoyed our tea, we'll have to get a move on, and driving fast through Hine and Exeter at this time of the day will be tricky.'

'I can—'

'—drive just as well as I can. I don't doubt it. But we'll leave the proof for some other occasion. Sugar?'

135

'No, thank you. And not much milk.'

'They've brought you cucumber sandwiches. I suppose you wouldn't swap them for my cress?'

'Help yourself. You're paying.'

'Austin's paying. I'm on business of his. You're having tea on him. Could you tell me why your children aren't with you?'

'Roberta said she'd be aunt. I don't have to worry, because the twins know what they like to do, and they'll tell her.'

'Not a bad summary of modern child-rearing methods.' He handed her a magazine. 'Read that, will you, while I finish going through these papers?'

Turning the pages of the magazine, she found her attention diverted by the entrance of a tall, good-looking man of about fifty. He sat down and ordered tea, and she wondered when he gave a room number if he was the man Austin had mentioned. She had a vague feeling that she had seen him before, but if he had been one of the passengers on the ship that had brought her from Canada, she could not recall him.

After so delayed a start, she felt that Elva would have to wait some time at Exeter station. But when she saw the pace at which Oliver drove, silent and concentrated and taking no risks, she realised that they would be in time. They reached the station as the train was drawing in.

136

'I'm going to wait out here,' Oliver said. 'You go and see if you can pick Elva out of the crowd.'

He watched her go, small, neat, graceful, and wondered with some apprehension what she would make of life from now on. Her school had handed her over to her father and her father had handed her over to Paul Brisson. It was clear that she had married him in the hope of finding security. She was self-reliant up to a point, but she lacked the kind of toughness that women like Elva and Roberta had. She seemed very young, very small, very vulnerable to be thrown into the world with two children.

Jeanne, not tall enough to see over heads, decided to stand beside the barrier past which passengers were beginning to stream. She had to wait some time. Only in the last group did she discern a tall figure she at once recognised as Elva. Studying her as she came near, she understood Roberta's anxiety to instil some elements of dress sense. Elva, who had good looks of a dark, heavy kind, was wearing creased trousers, sandals, a white cotton shirt and a navy blue cardigan. Her hair, shoulder-length, was dragged back and secured with a large plastic clip. The clothes, together with her upright, poised bearing and down-to-earth air, made Jeanne think of pictures she had seen of young revolutionaries.

She had no difficulty in recognising Jeanne.

137

'Hello, Jeanne. Not much changed after all these years,' she said as they met. 'Have you grown at all?'

'A little. How are you, Elva?'

They began to walk to the exit, Elva slightly in advance to elbow a way through the crowd.

'Oliver came with me—he drove me,' Jeanne said. 'He's waiting outside.'

'What's he doing down here?'

'He and Austin are here on business—something to do with something that Austin's building in Rocksea.'

Elva frowned.

'They're not going to be a nuisance, are they? I didn't think it was wise to let Oliver have the run of his room, and I told Roberta so. But apparently he made it a take-it-or-leave-it arrangement.'

Her voice was low-pitched, its tone in keeping with her appearance—sensible, unemphatic.

'Did you bring your children?' she asked.

'No. Roberta offered to look after them.'

'And you let her?'

'Yes.'

'What courage. Do you and Paul write to one another, or is everything quite finished?'

'He writes, mostly to the children. I answer questions about them.'

'No hope of a reconciliation?'

'No, none.'

Elva swung the suitcase she was carrying

138

from one hand to the other.

'I've got another case in the luggage van,' she said. 'There's no need for you to come through this crowd—I'll meet you outside.'

Jeanne, going out into the sunshine, saw Oliver talking to a woman and decided to wait at the entrance. She gave an appraising glance at the model suit, the beautiful handbag and matching shoes, and felt that a woman who could afford to spend so much on her appearance should bring her ideas on fashion up to date; it was not smart, today, to look so all-of-a-piece. She wondered, without much curiosity, who she was.

Oliver, passing the waiting period standing beside his car idly watching the people coming out of the station, had been roused by a voice at his shoulder.

'Mr Hobart?'

He turned. He saw a woman of about forty, slim, blonde and he would have added beautiful if her make-up had been toned down. In the few seconds before she spoke again, he attempted to adopt Austin's instant method of filing women: open-air, drawing room, or bar? This woman, he decided, fell into the last category; he could see her on a high stool in an expensive bar, with an expensive drink in front of her.

'You don't know me,' she said. 'I was waiting in the taxi queue and someone saw you and mentioned your name, so I thought I'd come over and introduce myself. I'm Maureen Selby. Maurice's wife.'

For some moments surprise, and the confused impressions in his mind, kept him silent. He thought it a pity that on an occasion such as this, there were polite forms to be observed, so that the one question which sprang to his mind could not be uttered: why on earth had she married him?

For he remembered Maurice Selby, and knew him to be a cold humourless man, hard to get on with. Why should a woman like this, who surely had a wide choice, pick a man like Selby? The most obvious reason seemed to be money; Selby had it, and she certainly spent it. That crocodile handbag and those matching shoes hadn't been given away.

He found his tongue.

'Yes. Oliver Hobart. How do you do?'

Despite himself, his tone was less than warm. She smiled.

'Let's start off right,' she suggested. 'Don't blame me for anything Maurice does. I came all the way across the road to ask you how much you know about this fuss that's going on over Parson's House.'

'I don't know much—that's to say, I don't know anything that everybody in Rocksea doesn't know. Mr Quinter has left the job.'

'That's why Maurice has sent me down here. There's a new firm of builders taking on the job tomorrow and he wants me to keep an eye

140

on them. I'm not clear what I'm expected to do. If they want to see ghosts, they'll see ghosts, won't they?'

'Are you going to stay in Exeter?'

'Worse. Much worse. I'm to stay at Rocksea. Maurice says the hotel's comfortable, but I don't believe it. Do you know it?'

'Yes. It's very good.'

'If it isn't, I'll go back to London and the builders can go to hell.'

He was getting her into focus. Beneath her free-and-easy manner—one which old Mrs Datchet would have termed bold—she had a dissatisfied, almost a defeated look. But beneath that he thought he detected a stubborn streak; if she went after anything, he decided, she would put up a hard fight to get it.

She was going to Rocksea, and he could have driven her to the hotel—but he could not bring himself to make the suggestion. She was in the enemy camp.

'Any chance of your dropping into the hotel for a drink?' she asked. 'Not now; I suppose you're here to meet somebody. But I don't know a soul down here and I'm not looking forward to seeing nobody but builders. What's so special about Parson's House, for God's sake? Why couldn't Maurice have sold it to his brother years ago? All he's done is sell the house in London, though I'd made it clear that I didn't want to come and live here.'

He had no comment to make, so said

141

nothing.

'It's no use talking to you about the house,' she said resignedly. 'Your grandfather built it and your mother lived in it and so you've got a special feeling for it. But Maurice never got over leaving it, and now I'm going to be stuck in it. Why does everything have to happen at once?'

'Did everything happen at once?'

'Yes. I had a job in an art gallery. The owners were Americans. A couple of months ago, they sold it, and it's being turned into an art school. That meant that my excuse for staying in London was gone. That meant that Maurice decided to sell our house and live down here. That meant that I got shipped down here to sit on the site and keep the spooks away from the workmen. Are you going to let me sit alone at that hotel every evening, or are you going to be friendly and take a drink off me? That is, if you're staying here—but you don't live here, do you?'

'Not usually. But I'm at Rocksea on business, so I'm staying at the cottage next door to Parson's House.'

'You own it, don't you?'

'Yes.'

'Is it far from the hotel?'

'Ten minutes' walk.'

'Then you've no excuse. Will you come?'

'You won't be lonely. A friend of mine named Austin Parkes is staying there.'

142

'Then come and see him, and I'll join you. Goodbye—for now.'

She left him. He watched her get into a taxi and drive away, and then brought his mind back to his own affairs. Looking across to the station entrance, he saw Elva and Jeanne coming towards the car, and walked over to meet them.

'Hello, Elva. Nice to see you.' He took the suitcases from her. 'What's in these—rocks?' he asked.

'Books. Papers. I've got work to do. Isn't it odd that Jeanne hasn't changed at all?'

'I don't know about odd. It's surprising, in some ways,' he said, putting the cases into the luggage compartment. 'All that experience—marriage, children, divorce—and she's come out of it all by that same door wherein she went. Not a scar to be seen. You'd better sit in front, Elva; you've got longer legs.' He closed the doors and took his place at the wheel. 'Is this a break in the middle of the Crusades, or is your job with the professor finished?'

'The research part of it's finished. I've got to sort out my findings.'

'Any idea what you'll do next? That is, after an interval for swimming and sun bathing.'

'I'm going up to Edinburgh to work with Lord Glentarn on a book he's writing about Holyrood Palace. It's been done before—the subject, I mean—but, as he pointed out, not by him. He claims to have some family papers

143

that give details that have never been published, not to say known. That's a claim made, of course, by numbers of people before they embark on a work of this kind. It's not always substantiated, but it looks well on the dust-jackets. Have you read many books on the subject?'

'No. But I made a study of it when I was about sixteen and fell madly in love with the Headmaster's daughter. Scottish, name of Shona, and with no time for anybody who didn't know the history of her homeland. I found a guide book on Holyrood Palace and learned it practically by heart, and poured facts into her ears whenever I got her alone on the games field. I'd only got halfway through when she left me for a weed who claimed he was descended from Macbeth.'

'What facts do you remember?' Elva asked, brushing aside the love interest.

'Oh, the usual. Abbey built in 1128, reconstructed in I think 1464, destroyed by the English round about 1560 and reconstituted as the Chapel Royal in 1672. How's that?'

'Very impressive. Any more?'

'One very important recent fact: this Lord Glentarn is a notorious womaniser, in case you haven't heard. You might find yourself fending him off with a claymore.'

'He won't bother me,' Elva said, with a confidence which Jeanne could not help feeling was entirely justified. Heavy in looks, she thought, and heavy in hand. She was beginning to see why there had been such harmony among the holiday children. Elva and Paul had kept the balance steady. Paul had been the one who arranged time-tables, estimated risks, planned or vetoed plans. Elva had been proof against emotional approaches, contributing her own brand of solid sense to whatever was going on. She damped down Roberta's impetuosity and Austin's flippancy. Now she would undoubtedly apply effective deterrents to the amorous Lord Glentarn.

She heard Oliver addressing her.

'You ought to know something about Holyrood, Jeanne. There was a strong French connection.'

'All I know from my history,' she said, 'is that Charles the First of England was crowned there.'

'And there's a blood stain somewhere—Rizzio's?' Oliver asked.

'That,' Elva said, 'is one of the things that Lord Glentarn claims to have inside knowledge on. We shall see.'

'Speaking of seeing,' Oliver said, 'did you see me talking to a woman outside the station? Guess who. Mrs Selby. Wife of Maurice.'

'Wife? I didn't realise he was married,' Elva said.

'He married about a year ago.'

'From the look of her, I'd say she was much younger than her husband. Isn't he in his

145

sixties?'

'No. He was a few years older than David. David was fifty-one; Maurice must be about fifty-five. She's going to stay at Cristall's. She's been sent down by her husband to see how the new lot of workmen get on at Parson's House. It's being done up and then they're going to live in it.'

'What happened to the old lot of workmen?'

'They left. Maurice sacked them.'

'Why?'

'You tell her, Jeanne,' Oliver said over his shoulder.

Jeanne told her. It did not sound a reasoned narrative. It began with rumours, took in Suni and Suji, glanced off Boris and ended with the story of Mr Quinter and his initial dismissal of ghostly manifestations. Elva listened without interrupting, her expression, as always, giving no clue to her reactions. When Jeanne came to a rather lame halt, she spoke thoughtfully.

'Doesn't sound like Rocksea,' she commented. 'Have you any idea where the rumours started?'

'If we knew that, we'd know which came first, the curate or the egg,' Oliver said. 'I'm sorry for poor Quinter. I was sure the ghost was going to find him unpromising material— but he went the way of the others. Now there's a new lot, with Mrs Selby to tell them to pay no attention to tall tales. Let's see what happens.'

Elva said nothing; Oliver guessed that she was feeding the facts into her built-in computer and would offer no solution until the answer came through.

When they arrived at the cottage, Jeanne thought her manner with the twins both sensible and successful. She allowed them their full quota of staring, and then fetched from her room two books she had brought for them—no narrative, only pictures.

'Don't look at them now,' she advised. 'Take them to bed with you. The pictures are all about the same little boy, and when you've finished one book, you can change over and read the other.'

Never reluctant to get into bed for their reading session, tonight they got through teeth-brushing and prayers at record speed. Closing the door on them, Jeanne went into the kitchen and embarked on the final preparations for dinner. She had no sooner finished laying the table when she heard the snuffling of dogs and the loud admonitions that invariably heralded the arrival of Lady Cressing. The three dogs appeared in the doorway; behind them, holding the leashes firmly, looking not unlike a charioteer, came their owner. She put up her free hand in a commanding gesture.

'No, Jeanne my dear, don't stop whatever it is you're doing. I'm not here to intrude or interrupt. I just looked in to say a word of greeting to Elva—has she arrived? Yes, there you are, Elva. How nice, how very nice to have you with us.'

Elva stooped to disentangle Duke from the three leashes, took them into her own grasp, wound them round the mudscraper outside the door and led the visitor through the archway to where Roberta, Austin and Oliver were seated round a table on which were drinks and a bowl of nuts. They rose and brought an extra chair, and Lady Cressing sank thankfully into it.

'You all look so comfortable, so well-arranged, such a happy, happy group,' she said, looking round her. 'I wish Lorna could see you all. She—Yes, sherry, thank you, Oliver. I don't have to ask if it's dry; I know how well you treat your guests. May I help myself to some of those delicious nuts? Thank you. Jeanne, why do they let you do all the work?'

'This is the usual form,' Roberta explained. 'We all do what we like doing. We like sitting here and drinking and waiting for dinner, and Jeanne likes being given a drink, and contributes to the conversation when she feels like it. As I'm the present part-owner of this cottage, I'm part-owner of the dinner. Why don't you stay and share it?'

'My dear'—Lady Cressing spoke with genuine feeling—'that's really very nice of you. That's the kind of thing a silly old woman like myself appreciates—being asked to join the young people. But I can't, thank you all the

148

same. I told poor old Trotter I wouldn't be more than ten minutes, and she gets terribly fussed if I keep meals waiting. What I'd like to ask Elva before I go is what she thinks of this ghost situation we're in. Have you seen the sightseers in the road, Elva? As I came past them just now, I said to myself: "Now Elva will view the matter with her usual detachment and good sense." You see, Elva, you're one of the few people I know who seems to be blessed with a total lack of imagination. I say blessed, you notice. Imagination is said to be a desirable quality, but I've never thought so. It's all right for writers and playwrights and people of that kind, they need it, I daresay, but I think it leads normal people astray. I'd much rather be without any. How often do you hear people saying "You mustn't let your imagination run away with you?" As a child, I never heard anything else. Elva, now, is never run away with. Now, Elva my dear, will you please tell me whether I'm to believe that Parson's House is haunted, or whether those who say it is, have—here we are again, you can't get away from it—let their imaginations run away with them?'

'My conclusions won't help you,' Elva answered. 'In a situation like this, people react according to their degree of credulity. Do you, yourself, believe in ghosts?'

'I keep an open mind.'

'That means you've never cared to answer

149

the question.'

'How can anybody answer it,' Lady Cressing asked, 'if they've, so to speak, never been put to the test?'

'Like Mr Quinter,' Oliver said. 'He was a firm non-believer. Right up to the last time he went into the house, he was convinced that his workmen had—'

'—let their imagination run away with them,' trumpeted Lady Cressing. 'So if I say that I don't believe in ghosts, which at this moment I most certainly do not, I might find myself in a position in which I should have to change my mind. Which do you think came first, Elva—the rumours, or the ghosts?'

'The rumours,' Elva answered unhesitatingly.

There was a pause—rare in any group which included Lady Cressing. Nor was she the first to break the silence.

'You think,' Oliver asked, 'that the rumours were started deliberately?'

'Yes, undoubtedly.' Elva spoke firmly. 'It's true that I can take an objective view; I'm a late-comer and I haven't seen or heard any of the people who claim, or think, or believe there's something supernatural in the house. But there seems to me too much evidence, too many people experiencing too much in too short a time. When a house gets a reputation for being haunted, the evidence is usually scanty, thinly-spread, with the scoffers far

150

outnumbering the convinced. The fact that an entire section of workmen were affected to a degree that made them give up their job, seems to me to point to some kind of deliberate preparation. The rumours must, I think, have been quite specific: the men were told what to expect.'

'But Elva'—Lady Cressing spoke earnestly—'I spoke to some of them. More down-to-earth men you never saw. And they were *frightened*.'

'I've just told you they were. Suggestion is a very subtle art. You asked me for my opinion, and I'm giving it to you: I think that the rumours were started deliberately in a place from which it was known that they would spread quickly, and fed systematically until a large number of people were persuaded into believing them.'

'I'll lay money on that,' Austin said. 'How about you, Roberta?'

'I'm keeping my money. I was the one Mr Quinter came to see in the first place. He was a sane, solid citizen and if he said someone pulled his scarf out of his hand, who's to say he was lying? I told Jeanne that I think I can see Lorna sitting on the terrace at nights, sometimes, and if the things that people said were happening inside the house hadn't been hurtful things, like falling downstairs, I'd have been prepared to believe that Lorna was still around. As it is, I feel as though I'm sitting on

151

both sides of the fence, so how can I lay bets?'

'For myself,' Lady Cressing said, 'I feel far less confused than I did, and I'm grateful to have been able to clear my head. The thing that reassures me is that all of you, except Elva, have been through the house and found everything there absolutely normal. No, Oliver, most certainly not another drink, thank you. I must hurry away.' She rose. 'I wish I could invite you all to dinner one evening, but it would kill poor old Trotter. What I would like very much is to give you a nice cold supper. Shall we say tomorrow, if you're all free? Jeanne, you have no need to worry about the children. If you will leave some sandwiches for Trotter, she'll come over and baby-sit; she'll love it. Are you all free? Good. Then shall we say eight o'clock? Good, good, good.' She went to the door and waited for Oliver to hand her the dogs' leashes. 'I shall look forward to seeing you all. Goodbye, goodbye.'

'And there,' Austin said, as she left, 'is the solution to the baby-sitting difficulty. Why didn't we think of Trotter?'

They cleared away the glasses, emptied the ash trays and sat down to dinner. They ate liver pâté, veal with a delicate sauce, and biscuits with a variety of cheeses. The meal over, Jeanne as usual was off duty, and the others cleared away, loaded the dish-washing machine and made coffee. It was almost eleven when Austin rose to go, and invited Oliver to go with him for a nightcap.

They walked slowly over the bridge; below them, the lights of cars flashed by and the lights of the town twinkled. Above was a sky bright with stars. The breeze that almost always blew on the promontory lessened as they descended to town level and walked up the hotel drive.

'Guess who's staying here,' Oliver said.

'Someone I know?'

'Someone we both know well by name, but have never met.'

'Give up.'

'Mrs Selby.'

'Wife of Maurice?'

'Yes.'

'Here, in Rocksea?'

'Yes. Alone. He sent her down to keep an eye on the new lot of workmen. She's not looking forward to it. She regards this place as outside the civilised perimeter.'

'What's she like?'

'You'll see, if she's around when we go in. Attractive in a sort of rather obvious way.'

'Young?'

'No. About forty, I'd say. I think you're going to see a lot of her.'

'How am I supposed to decode that?'

'I mean she's lonely. She asked me over for a drink. She's looking for company. I offered her yourself.'

'Nice of you. I'm not quite the type that

153

lonely women go for. And didn't I hear someone say that Selby's insanely jealous?'

'What could he find to be jealous about in a place like Rocksea?'

'The other hotel guests. All those workmen. Me, if he finds me trying to make her less lonely. Or, knowing that he's jealous, will she keep men at a distance?'

Oliver did not answer for some moments.

'No,' he said at last. 'Somehow, I've got a feeling she's found a way round Maurice.'

They had reached the hotel entrance. A page sprang forward to open one of the doors.

'It sounds to me,' Austin said as they went in, 'as though you've made a study of her.'

'Study? No. But she surprised me. I detest him so much that I couldn't imagine any attractive woman marrying him. I can't understand why she did, unless it was money.'

'In spite of which, you think she's nice?'

'No. In the sense you mean it, she's not nice at all. But there she is. You can make up your own mind. Do you want to be introduced?'

Austin, after a lightning survey, spoke with decision.

'Yes. I do.'

'Then here we go.'

It occurred to them both, as they crossed the hall, that Mrs Selby's fear of loneliness had been more than realised. The lounge they were approaching, clearly visible through wide glass doors, was extremely large, beautifully-furnished—and almost completely deserted. In a far corner sat a white-haired couple writing postcards. In a distant alcove a man, middle-aged, well-dressed and good-looking—Oliver recognised him as the man who had come into the reading room for tea—sat absorbed in a book. In another alcove, Mrs Selby was seated on a sofa beside Mr Cristall. The silence, the sober atmosphere made an almost painful contrast to the lively scene in the restaurant which opened on the other side of the hall. It was, as always, full. The diners were for the most part formally-dressed; those who wanted a cheaper meal went next door to the Lion, where they could get roast beef and the celebrated Cristall salad. Like the restaurant, the pub was invariably filled to capacity.

Mr Cristall, seeing Austin and Oliver as they entered, rose and went a few steps to meet them, his portly, florid appearance a good advertisement for the fare he provided. He spoke with a broad Devon accent.

'Good to see you,' he said. 'Come and meet a lady.'

'We've already met,' Mrs Selby said. 'At least, I've met Mr Hobart.'

'Then you must meet his friend, Mr Parkes. A few minutes before you came through the door, Oliver, Mrs Selby was telling me she didn't see much stimulating company here—and now look! Two of you, one a fellow-guest.'

'You're a genius,' Mrs Selby told him lazily.

155

She was leaning back against the sofa cushions, wearing a long, dark green dress, a light scarf across her shoulders. 'I've been sitting here since dinner. So have the two old Australians sitting over there sending postcards back to the bush. So has the man with the book.'

Mr Cristall had waved the two men to chairs. A waiter had appeared with coffee and sandwiches. Mr Cristall bowed.

'With my compliments,' he said. 'And now I've got to go up to bed; I'm staying here tonight, but I'm going to be very busy tomorrow—I've got to be in Exeter by ten thirty.' He turned away and then paused. 'The gentleman over there reading a book,' he told Mrs Selby, 'is one of my oldest customers, so if you would allow—'

'No. No introductions, thank you, Mr Cristall. My husband's middle name is Othello and I like to be discreet. Goodnight, and thank you for being so kind.'

Mr Cristall walked to the lift, and Mrs Selby began to pour out coffee.

'He's been telling me the history of Rocksea,' she said. 'Not only places, but people.'

'He's very well-known,' Oliver said. 'Not only here, but in London. If you want to know anything about anybody here, just ask him.'

She handed him his coffee.

'What exactly is going on in this house I'm supposed to be coming to live in?' she asked.

156

'Mr Cristall said quite definitely that it's haunted. Do you believe that?'

'No. We're anti-ghost,' Oliver said. 'We borrowed the key from the builder and went over the house, and nothing happened to us.'

'Who's us?' she asked.

'Austin and myself and two of the girls who used to come to Parson's House for their school holidays about ten years ago.'

'School . . .' There was a subtle, momentary change in Mrs Selby's expression. It was gone so swiftly that Oliver thought he must have imagined it. 'Oh yes, I know. That was something Maurice never got over—he said the house shouldn't have been used for what he called commercial purposes. But that was long before I came on the scene. Did the two girls come down specially to see the haunt?'

'No. They've rented my cottage.'

'Names?'

'Roberta Murray, and a French girl just back from Canada.'

'How long have they rented the cottage for?'

'As long as they want it. I'm using my room whenever I need it.'

'Very convenient.' She dismissed the subject. 'Will you do something for me?'

'If I can.'

'The new builder is going to meet me at the house tomorrow at eleven. Could you be there? Both of you, if you're free.'

'I'm not,' Austin said. 'I've got two meetings.

You're free, aren't you, Oliver?'

Oliver thought that he was. Austin, after glancing at Mrs Selby for permission, reached for the sandwiches.

'There's whisky in my room, if anybody thinks it's a good idea,' he said.

'Not me, thank you.' Mrs Selby gave a long, unrestrained yawn. 'I'm going to bed.' She glanced at the diamond-surrounded watch on her wrist. 'I'm feeling exhausted—it's all this excitement. God knows how long I'll be able to stand it.'

They saw her to the lift. Oliver waited for Austin to finish the sandwiches and then said he would go home. Austin walked to the end of the drive with him.

'Want to know what I think of her?' he asked.

'Yes.' Oliver smiled. 'Outdoor, drawing room, or bar?'

'Bar. Very Ritzy bar. Attractive, as you said. A man's woman, not a woman's woman. Sexy, which you didn't say but which you implied. And something else which may have escaped your notice: she's after something, and it isn't us. You agree?'

'Yes. Go on.'

'There's no more, except one curious thing: did you see her react when you mentioned Jeanne and Roberta?'

'Yes. I thought I'd imagined it.'

'You didn't. She went tense for a couple of

158

seconds. Why?'

'I don't know.'

'Nor do I, but it would be interesting to try and find out. Will you go and meet her at the house tomorrow?'

'Yes. I'd like to see what Quinter's successor is like. Good night. Even if it isn't us she's after, how about locking your door?'

'No need. I'm a man's man, not a woman's man. Good night.'

CHAPTER SIX

Oliver slept late on the following morning. Waking, he put on a dressing gown and went downstairs. There was nobody in the kitchen. He cooked himself a substantial breakfast, and while waiting for his toast to be ejected from the toaster, looked round the room and noted approvingly its cleanliness and order. Not thus, he told himself, had it appeared before the advent of Jeanne. A place for everything— there was nothing new about that. But everything in its place—that had not been known since his mother died.

He was finishing his third egg when Austin came in. He raised his eyebrows at the sight of Oliver still in his dressing gown.

'Overslept?' he enquired.

'No. Just slept. I thought you had meetings

159

to attend.'

'I'm on my way. I looked in to ask whether you found any snags in those papers I asked you to look over.'

'No. None. I'm not as keen as you are on this architect fellow.'

'He's all right. He's got an unfortunate manner, that's all.'

'That's not all. He's un-cooperative and he's pig-headed. Coffee?'

Austin hesitated, looked at his watch and then got a cup and saucer and pulled a chair to the table.

'Girls down on the beach?' he asked.

'Jeanne and Roberta are. Elva's still in her room—I heard her moving round.'

Austin cut two slices of bread, found them too thick to fit into the toaster, and buttered them instead.

'This new lot of builders,' he remarked, 'are bound to have made enquiries about why the last lot melted away. What's to prevent them from becoming infected?'

'They're outsiders, for one thing. And Exeter's a city, so they'll probably be more sophisticated, and write off Quinter's men as superstitious yokels. And remember they've got Mrs Selby's eye on them.'

'Speaking of Mrs Selby, I found out a bit more about that picture gallery she used to work in.'

'Have you talked to her?'

160

'No. She hadn't come down when I left. It was old Cristall. We had breakfast together. He told me that Mrs Selby had nothing to do with picture-buying or selecting; all she had to do was sell pictures that the owners hadn't managed to get rid of in America. Mediocre stuff, he said.'

'How does he know?'

'First, because he always knows everything; next, because his restaurant isn't far from the gallery and buyers come in now and then.' He reached for the coffee pot, cut two more slices of bread, thinner than the last, and put them into the toaster. 'He's certainly a local news bulletin. When I left, he was telling the two Australians about Rocksea's haunted house. The fellow who was reading the book came down just as I came away so he'll be regaled with the story too. It'll spread from Devon to Darwin. Any more coffee?'

'No.'

'I thought I left some in the pot.'

'You did. For me. You had your breakfast— you said so.'

Austin went to the refrigerator, took out a bottle of milk, poured a large glassful and drank it.

'Got to go,' he said. 'I'll drop in here for a drink before we all go over to Boris's. I'm not looking forward to this cold supper, are you?'

'No. I can't think why the hell we didn't see it coming, and dodge. It was the same when we

161

were young, remember? Warm invitation to a cold supper which turned out to be very thin slices of ham and a cornflour mould made in the shape of a rabbit. I'm not abusing hospitality, but six healthy teenagers, if invited, have to be filled. I could never get my mother to agree.'

'Remember those parlour games she used to make us play? You don't think she'll start on those tonight, do you?'

'I hope not.' He pushed aside his plate, rose and walked to the door. 'See you some time this evening.'

'Right. Don't get too involved with Mrs Selby. She—Oh, hello, Jeanne.'

Jeanne had come up from the beach, and after saying good morning, was opening the door of the refrigerator.

'It's lovely down there,' she said. 'I've come up for the twins' milk. It was so hot that I left it to keep cool.'

There was no milk in the refrigerator. With a puzzled frown, she bent to look at the lower shelves—and then she saw the almost empty bottle on the table.

'Oh Lord,' Austin muttered. 'Oh crumbs. Oh madre mia. It was Oliver's fault,' he explained. 'He wouldn't share his coffee, and I was thirsty and . . . Look, I'll go round to the shop and bring you back—'

'No, you won't,' Oliver broke in. 'You're late for your meeting as it is. If it's necessary, I'll go

162

and get some milk.'

Jeanne turned to look at him.

'You think it's not necessary?' she asked.

He drew his dressing gown round him and tightened the cord.

'I wouldn't like to do your children out of their milk supply,' he said. 'I merely thought it wouldn't hurt them to wait until the milkman came. How about taking them down a drink of orange juice instead? Nice change from all that milk, I would have thought.'

'They don't like fruit juice.'

'Too bad.'

Austin made an attempt to pour oil.

'It was all my fault, as I said. Oliver was having his breakfast and—'

'I can see that.' She threw a glance round the dirty cups, the egg-spattered saucepan, the greasy plate, the napkin crumpled and left on the chair. 'Were you going to leave everything like this?' she asked Oliver.

'Habit,' he explained. 'I'm used to being alone here, and it's hard to remember that standards have risen.'

'It is easy to put things into the dish-washing machine.'

'That's what I thought. Anything else?'

She made no reply. She took the milk bottle from the table, went out and closed the door with a bang.

'So small but so fierce,' Austin said admiringly.

163

'So young but so damned fussy. You can see why Paul spent all his time in the jungle.'

Austin was clearing the table.

'When you come to think of it,' he said, 'it's a change to have a nice, tidy house. All Jeanne's trying to do is—'

There was no point in continuing. Oliver was on his way upstairs.

When he came down again, he was in shirt and jeans. He walked across to Parson's House, found nobody there and sat down to wait on the bench on which his mother had so often sat, hands at rest on her lap, eyes looking serenely over the sea. Like her father, she had loved this view. Oliver had not been surprised at her wish to be buried at sea. Better in its depths, he thought now, than under a headstone in Hine cemetery, or a handful of ashes sprinkled over the cottage garden.

He was roused, as at the station in Exeter, by the sound of Mrs Selby's voice. Before he could rise, she had seated herself beside him.

'No builder?' she asked.

'Not yet.'

'He's late. A bad start. I didn't really expect to see you. I hoped you'd come, but what's the use of getting friendly? Once Maurice puts in an appearance, you'll keep out of his way. I don't blame you. If ever I do come and live here, I won't be bothered by his friends, because he hasn't any. Even Mr Cristall couldn't hide the fact that he dislikes him.' She

164

turned her restless gaze on the sea. 'Your mother liked it here, didn't she?'

'Yes.'

'But she was away from Rocksea for a long time, wasn't she? Your father wasn't a Devon man?'

'No. They met in a hospital in Chester. He was a surgeon. I was born in Chester. She came back here when my father died.'

'She was very good-looking, wasn't she?'

'Yes.'

'And young when she came back to the cottage, and widowed, with a small boy. And David watched her, sorry for her at first and then sorry for himself because she didn't give him any encouragement.'

Oliver smiled.

'How do you know that?'

'By guessing that her son must be like her. You're not what I'd call the responsive type. So your mother knew that David was pining up here, but she went on pulling up weeds and snipping off rose heads, and never so much as glanced up from under her wide-brimmed straw hat. And behind David there was Maurice—just as there is today, only he's not watching David, he's watching me, and you know it and you prefer not to get involved. How old were you when your mother and David married?'

'Eleven.'

'Did you guess you might be getting a stepfather?'

'No. I'd got used to thinking of him as a neighbour.' He paused. 'They were very happy together. It was a good marriage.'

'Will you believe me when I tell you that I tried to stop Maurice from turning her out of the house when his brother died?'

'Yes. I don't suppose anybody could have stopped him. He'd waited a long time.' He looked at her curiously. 'Do you really prefer London to'—he made a vague gesture—'all this?'

'I do. I'll admit it's a lovely house, but I'd trade it for a semi-detached in a Chelsea square. If I can get out of living in it, I will. I've thought a lot about your mother since I came here. She was lucky—she married the goodie. She was happy. She was in love. Have you ever been in love?'

'Now and then. Nothing serious.' And before he could stop himself, he added: 'Have you?'

'Yes. I caught it late, and I caught it badly.'

He might, he thought afterwards, have put the question he found so difficult to answer: why had she married Selby? The hint of passion in the tone in which she had spoken made it clear that her words did not relate to her husband. But there was no opportunity for more conversation; the builder had arrived and Mrs Selby had risen and walked a few paces to meet him.

166

'Mr Dent?'

'That's right.' He put out a hand. 'Pleased to meet you.'

A greater contrast to Mr Quinter, Oliver thought, could scarcely have been found. This was Reginald Dent, the son of Dent and Son. He had heard that they were prosperous builders; the extent of their prosperity was evident in the clothes and demeanour of the man shaking hands with Mrs Selby. He was about thirty, with long, fair hair framing a fox-like face. He wore black jeans cut in the latest mode, a silk shirt with a colourful and complicated pattern over it, a hand-knitted cardigan with his initials worked over the breast pocket. His voice was one which Oliver thought of as plummy. His air was one of conferring favours. He took no notice of Oliver.

'First thing we have to do,' he told Mrs Selby, 'is fix up the little matter of transport. I came in my car, of course, but you'll have to give me the OK to hire a mini-bus for my men, or they'll waste half their day coming and going.' He turned to look at the house. 'Nice little place. I know a good bit about architecture, so I can spot some things that could've been done better, but on the whole it's come off pretty well, considering. That's more than you can say about the other houses in this road. I'd like to pull 'em all down and start again, if you follow me. You've got the keys, I suppose?'

Mrs Selby opened her handbag, took them out and gave them to him. He went with a leisurely, hip-swinging gait to the front door and after a moment's trial, found the right key and opened it.

'Shall we?' he called to Mrs Selby over his shoulder.

'Will you come too?' she asked Oliver.

He followed her into the hall. Mr Dent did all the talking. Producing from a pocket a sheet of paper, he went from room to room, reading as he went.

'Hall . . . light green walls. There are lots of light greens, you know. You'll have to specify. My wife—she's outside now, in the car—likes a touch of avocado. She says it gives a nice finish. She ought to know—she was in the decorating business. She could give you a lot of tips about bringing this place up to date. Drawing room . . . dining room . . . study. Which would that be? Oh yes, I see. Upstairs—I'll nip up in a moment. New window frames, glass in the balconies, take down small wooden gate—that'll be the one I saw as I came in, top of the path, right? Roof . . . gutters . . .' He folded the paper. 'It's all fairly clear, except the colours,' he told Mrs Selby. 'You'll be around, I suppose, if I need you?'

'I'll stay as long as my husband thinks it necessary. He didn't mention any dates.'

'Not a bad idea to stick around for the first

couple of weeks,' Mr Dent said. 'The client ought to show an interest, get to know one or two of the men, chat 'em up; makes 'em feel it's all more personal, if you follow me. I'll go upstairs and take a look round. Mind if I go on my own?'

'Not at all.'

He left them in the hall. Mrs Selby walked slowly into the drawing room. Oliver, following, stood watching as she idly lifted dust sheets and glanced at the brocade covering the chairs.

'Good furniture,' she said, 'and lovely covers. How was it all those children didn't wreck the place?'

'In summer,' he told her, 'we hardly set foot indoors. The girls slept in this house, the boys slept in the cottage. It took very bad weather to prevent us from going out, but if we had to stay in, we all went down to the cottage. David rigged up a sort of gymnasium, and he put up easels and the girls used to paint, and at the end of the day he'd come down and see that we cleared things up.'

'The man who was at the hotel with you last night—is he the Austin Parkes who's giving away a lot of money to charities?'

'Yes.'

'I read about him in some paper or other. I thought he was older. You work for him?'

'Yes. As well as for other clients.'

They heard Mr Dent coming downstairs,

and went into the hall.

'That's the lot for now,' he told Mrs Selby. 'I'll get the men on the job tomorrow. You needn't worry about them staying on it. I know all about the last lot—ghosts popping out of paint pots and all that.' He gave a loud, high-pitched laugh. 'You always get a lot of superstition in a place like this.'

'The other builders were a London firm before they moved down here,' Mrs Selby informed him.

'So I was told. Pity they listened to the natives. If any of my men fall off ladders, I'll have 'em put through a breath test.' He put out his hand and gave her a hearty handshake. 'So long for now. Will you keep the keys, or will I?'

'I shan't be needing them.'

'Then I'll hang on to them.' He opened the front door. 'If there's anything—Oh, hello, Dot. Come on in. This is my wife,' he told Mrs Selby.

On the doorstep was a vision which Oliver later described as a strawberry soufflé. She was about the same age as her husband, plump, pretty and dressed in teen-age clothes. The overall effect was pink—revealing pink play suit, pink limbs, expensive pink sandals and pink-and-white striped beach bag.

'Oh Reg, you've been ages!' she said, and gave him a forgiving smile. 'You said you'd get it over in no time at all. You must be Mrs Selby. How do you do? So nice to meet you. I

170

always like to meet Reg's customers. And this'—she turned a coy smile on Oliver—'is your husband? How do you—'

'No. This is Mr Hobart,' Mrs Selby said. 'He lives next door.'

'Oh, next door? Next door *that* way'—she waved a hand, making her bracelets jangle—'or *that* way?'

'Down there,' Oliver said, and turned to Mrs Selby. 'Would you like me to run you back to the hotel?'

'Oh, *we'll* do that,' said Dot. 'There's loads and loads of room in the car. Isn't there, Reg?'

'Should be. Cost enough,' he said. 'We could've done with a smaller one, just Dot and me, but the old people like to be driven round, and they like to be comfortable, so I said if they paid the extra, I'd buy the bigger model.'

'It's a bit too big for a little place like this,' Dot complained. 'Once you get off the main road, there's no room to manoeuvre.'

'She knows what she's talking about,' Mr Dent told them. 'She's done a bit of racing in her time.'

'Oh, hardly any,' she said modestly. 'It was just that I had this boy friend, before I met Reg, and he had this racing car and he let me drive it.'

'Nerve enough for anything,' her husband explained. 'Well, Dot, we've got to get a move on. Coming, Mrs Selby?'

Mrs Selby thanked him and said that the

walk would do her good. The door closed behind the pair.

'You can write and tell your husband you won't be needed,' Oliver said. 'Dot's the one who's going to keep the builders on the job.'

'She's what used to be called a dish, isn't she? I've heard that plump pullets are tender, but this one's as tough as they come. I thought that cooing went out with bustles, but I suppose it keeps Reg titillated.'

'Are you going to look round upstairs?'

'No. What's the use? I suppose you're going to tell me that the view's even better from up there, but what does a view do for anybody? The only view I want is a view of a London street with people passing, with neighbours, with something going on all the time. Down here, I feel trapped. You don't understand that, do you?'

'No.'

'Well, it's true. I don't suppose your mother could have breathed in London. I can't breathe anywhere else.' She paused. 'Yes, I could, if you gave me a house like this one, looking over the sea as this one does. But it would have to be a warm sea, and I'd have to have warm sand to lie on and a cool drink where I could reach it. London—or a tropical island, either one. But not this, and not here.'

'Have you tried selling your husband the idea of the tropical island?'

'He'd laugh. No, he wouldn't; he'd sneer.

172

He doesn't laugh. Did David laugh?'

'Yes.'

'I wish I'd known him. Come on—let's go.'

He parted from her at the end of the road and walked thoughtfully back to the cottage. He felt sorry for her, but to his surprise he found that there was a small corner of his mind that harboured some compassion for Maurice Selby, who could not have found much satisfaction in living with a woman who hated him.

He entered the cottage to find Roberta on her way upstairs.

'Not swimming?' he asked.

'No. Later. What are you going to do?'

'Swim, change and join Austin for lunch in Exeter.'

'You wouldn't like a woman to pour out your coffee after lunch?'

'Not today. Where's Elva?'

'In her room.'

He changed, looked for and found a clean beach towel and went down to the beach. Duke came halfway up the path to meet him.

'I seem to have lost my dog,' he told Jeanne, spreading his towel beside her. 'He's grasped the fact that you're around more than I am. What's that game the twins are playing?'

'There's a giant in the castle they've built. It's got two gates.'

'Gates?'

'Use your imagination. Jo's a Frenchman

173

and Polly's an Englishman and they're guarding a gate each, to get the giant as he comes out.'

'He's coming out?'

'They don't know. But if he does, they're going to slice him up with their knives.'

'Knives?'

'Spades to you. You can be the giant if you like.'

'I don't like. I have something to say.'

'Yes?'

'An apology. I'm sorry I messed up your nice kitchen.'

'I'm sorry I fussed.'

'So am I. I always wondered whether I'd find a mission in life. I've found one: to see that you don't devote yourself entirely to twins and kitchens.'

'I love my children and I love cooking. Can't I do what I like doing?'

'Only so long as you preserve a balance. Everybody doesn't like order as much as you do, so when—as now—you're living with the disorderly, don't expect them to clear up all the mess they make. They don't notice it.'

'Why should it be good to paint tiles or do research, like Roberta and Elva, and not good to cook and look after children, like me?'

'I've never tried to work that one out. The point is that the four walls of a house, if you shut yourself up inside them, can be pretty confining.'

'Then if I can ever afford to have servants, and if the servants are good, I'll leave them to cook and clean while I do something else. What else, I don't know. I think that most parties are a terrible waste of time, talking to people you don't want to see again, listening to silly people saying silly things. You like to go out to dinner. I like to cook a perfect meal and see six, eight guests enjoying it. If you haven't got a home that you like to stay in, what have you got? Nowhere. Paul doesn't need a home; only a tent. But for me, I have only one gift, and that is to make a home, and that is what I am going to do. Somewhere, some time.'

'That's all right; go ahead. But don't wrap it round you like a cocoon. That's all. And now something else: Will you come out with me this evening and let me give you a drink before we have to go and eat cold ham with Boris?'

'Who will put the twins to bed?'

'We will, before we go. Elva and Roberta will be in the house until Trotter turns up. Austin will also be there. Does that calm your fears?'

'Yes.'

He rose.

'Good. There's time for a swim before I go and meet Austin. You used to be able to keep up with me from this rock to that one just being covered by the tide. Can you still do it?'

She kept up until they had almost reached the rock and then, with a breathless laugh, shook back her hair, turned on her back and fell away. He turned and swam back to her.

'Out of condition,' he said. 'Run to seed.'

They swam slowly back. The twins were shouting and waving their spades, which meant, Oliver said, that the giant had broken cover. He offered himself as reinforcements and was told that there was no need for assistance; the giant had been dealt with.

'Then I'll leave you to bury him,' he said, and picked up his towel. 'I'll call for you at six,' he told Jeanne.

When he drove away with her in the evening, he explained that his real object was to take her on a brief tour of the places they remembered in and round Rocksea. Many landmarks had gone. The narrow cart tracks over Rockcommon had been obliterated by lines of houses; the biggest of the farms was now a flourishing day school. The blacksmith had gone, with the ring of metal and the patient waiting horses.

'What happened to the family that lived on the other side of Rockcommon in that terrible little cottage?' Jeanne asked. 'There were nine, or was it ten children?'

'Ten. Their cottage was condemned and there was an almighty row—led by Boris—over where the children were to be housed. It would have been easy to parcel them out, but Boris fought that, and at last called in Austin. It was his first, so to speak, case. He knew more about the children than any of the authorities who were doing the arguing. He even knew the names of the ten children, as we all did, once. He discovered that Mum had a farmer brother in Hine who'd lost his wife and his interest in life. No children. If the poor fellow hadn't been sunk in gloom, he might have realised what he was letting himself in for—but he didn't come to until his barn was converted and the whole family installed. It's worked out very well. He's got eight strong young boys helping on the farm, and two nice nieces to walk to church with him on Sundays.'

'What happened to poor lame old Mrs Mayes?'

'Dead. Run over. Drunk driver. He got a prison sentence. When he got out, he married her daughter, but he must wish he'd stayed in prison, because she won't let him drink anything but water. Which reminds me that I haven't given you that drink I promised you.'

'I'd rather go on driving round.'

'So would I, but we'll both need a drink before facing Boris's supper. Especially if we're made to play guessing games after it.'

They got to the gate of Vistamar just as the small, thin, martial figure of Trotter was coming out. Jeanne got out of the car and went to embrace her; small as she was, she had to bend in order to reach the weather-beaten cheek.

'How are you, Trotter?'

'Same's usual, miss.' Her voice was piping, clear and firm. 'Can't complain. You look a treat. Pity about Master Paul, but I could've told you you wouldn't make a go of it. Too restless, he was. I'm just going over to sit with the babies.'

'I'll come with you.'

'Come on, then. Identical twins, can't tell t'other from which, Miss Opie says.'

Jeanne, searching her mind for a Miss Opie, remembered that Lady Cressing was not really Boris. Her parents had christened her Parthenope.

*　　　*　　　*

She was standing at the door of Vistamar, beckoning imperiously to Oliver.

'Come in, Oliver, will you? I want to talk to you.'

He left his car and walked to meet her.

'I wanted a word with you before the others came,' she said as they were on their way to the lofty, littered, dog-smelling drawing room which opened on to the patio. It was here that she spent all her days. It was cold in summer and arctic in winter, but the dogs could come and go freely. The furniture was a medley of the pieces which had been put into the house by her father—cheap, and chosen with a view to withstanding the assaults of the children— and the beautiful things she had brought with her when she returned to live in the house.

'Sit down,' she invited. 'No, not there, dear boy; how many times have I told you all that if you sit on a chair with a cushion on it, you must always look under the cushion for the dogs' bones.'

Oliver threw the bone into the patio and closed the door just in time to prevent the three dogs from entering.

'That's right; we don't want them inside when there are visitors,' Lady Cressing said. 'They take up too much room. People seem to think I ought to keep them outside all the time, which is absurd, because I like their company, though I do think sometimes that the room is beginning to have a faintly doggy smell. Pour yourself out a drink, Oliver. I'll take a small, very small sherry.'

He took it to her, but did not leave her chair. He stood looking down at her with a frown.

'There's something I want to talk to you about,' he said.

'Presently, presently, dear boy. You don't have to strike a pose like an inquisitor. Sit down.'

'In a moment. What I wanted to say—'

'It's probably the very thing I wanted to talk to you about. I wanted to tell you—'

'Let me tell you. The ghost rumours aren't the only ones that are circulating in this town. I was told by several people that you're about to

179

start a grandmothers' club.'

'Is it being talked about already? Oh Oliver, I'm delighted! The more people who get to know about it, the more grandmothers will come flocking to join. What else did they say?'

'That you're calling it the Fifth Wheel.'

'Yes. Isn't that apposite, as clever Elva would say? Most grandmothers are just that: fifth wheels. Nobody knows more about the women of this town than I do, and I've been studying the grandmother question—the grandmother problem—for some time. Some of them—the ones who have money—achieve a certain degree of independence, but having got it, don't know what to do with it. Others, poor things, have been rejected by the younger generation and see nothing of their grandchildren. Others have gone to live with their sons and daughters and grandchildren, but in most cases they're being used as the family drudge. So I said to myself: why not get them all together and turn them from grandmothers into *women*?'

'Why not indeed? But—'

'I know exactly what you're going to say. I've been waiting for you to come and say it.'

'Good. I'm going to say that in all the years I've known you, I understood—and my mother and David also understood—that you had never had any children. So—'

'—so how could I suddenly turn into a grandmother? Well, answer me this: if I

180

weren't a grandmother, how could I start a grandmothers' club? It would be absurd. I should lack the basic, the necessary qualification.'

'That's what I thought. So—'

'So how did I qualify? I didn't. I don't. And looking at most of the grandmothers I know, I've always been thankful that I escaped the role. But that doesn't prevent me from wanting to put the poor old things on their own feet. They've years and years of healthy life ahead, a lot of them, and nothing to use them for. So I—'

'Did you invent a son or a daughter?'

'Don't be absurd, Oliver. I invented nothing. All that was necessary was to stop Mr Cristall when I ran into him in the town one morning, and confide my little plan to him.'

'Didn't he express surprise at your suddenly becoming a grandmother?'

'He simply said he hadn't known that I was. To which I replied, not wishing to say anything that wasn't strictly true, that just because things hadn't turned out well in my own case, that needn't prevent me from trying to help women who had had better luck. I put it better than that, I think. He looked very touched. And of course, it was all round town in a moment—trust dear Mr Cristall for that. But I'm so pleased to hear that it's being talked about. People I've met have asked me about it, and I've told them about my plans, but if the question of my grandmotherhood came up, I simply said that I didn't care to discuss it. Which is true. I won't involve myself in details; once you start that kind of thing, you get into a great muddle.'

'What about Trotter?'

'Reliability itself, dear boy. She's all in favour, and she'll snub anybody who gets too curious. Her line is going to be that my secrets are safe with her. I'm so glad to be able to discuss it with you now. I wanted to ask if you would do for the grandmothers what you so kindly do for my other interests in Rocksea.'

'Straighten out the financial tangles?'

'If you would. After all, the fact of appointing a woman an honorary treasurer doesn't turn her into a financial wizard, does it?'

'From the evidence, no. How about club premises?'

'I was coming to that. You remember that years ago, Mrs Plume-Glover turned an old coach house of hers into a little cinema? She hasn't used it since she found it was easier to sit in her drawing room and look at films on television, so I—'

'You won't get anything out of Mrs Plume-Glover.'

'That's what everybody said. We all know she's notoriously miserly. But I saw, when I spoke to her about the club for grandmothers, that she was interested, and so I mentioned the coach house and dropped a hint—quite delicately—that she couldn't take it with her.'

'The coach house?'

'Don't be silly. Her money. The seed didn't fall on stony ground. We've got our club house and we've got a nice donation towards expenses. I think she's going to end by leaving quite a lot of it behind.'

'And having got the grandmothers, including your unqualified self, into the club, what do you all do?'

'Everything. We form fours for bridge. We choose companions for travel. We don't herd, but we make up teams to go on expeditions. We *learn*. I'm arranging speakers on history, politics and so on. Suni has promised to give us lessons on curry-making. I shall catch Elva before she goes, to give us a talk on the Crusades. And I shall get hold of our Member and ask him to give a talk on freedom, because you know, Oliver, however hard one tries to be liberal, you can't say it hasn't got into the wrong hands. All I'm doing is trying to give grandmothers back their identities—isn't that what those campaigners are hoping to do? But they're pulling against the current, because they're concerned with younger women, and most younger women have inescapable duties, especially if they're the mothers of young children, like dear Jeanne.'

'Won't your family be a little surprised to learn that you're a grandmother?'

183

'You mean my brothers and sisters? Fortunately, some of them are dead, and the rest, all but one, are scattered far and wide. The only brother within reach is not likely to come to Rocksea, and he's so absent-minded that he'd think he had forgotten when my children were born. I offered Trotter the choice of joining the club, or staying out, and she said she'd stay out. You must come and address us on finance, and Austin must give a talk about some of those poor refugees, and we'll take a collection. You do agree, Oliver, that I'm doing a good thing? I don't have to ask you for an assurance that you'll respect my little secret. I know you to be a rock of discretion.'

'Thank you.'

'And now that we've finished with that, I'm going to speak severely. I want to know whom you were talking to this morning in the garden of Parson's House.'

'Mrs Selby.'

'So I suspected, but I refused to believe it because I didn't dream that you, of all people, would behave in a friendly way towards her. You even—I was watching—went into the house with her.'

'Yes, I did.'

'You amaze me. You really do. Did she approach you and ask you to go with her?'

'Yes. She came down on the same train as Elva, and spoke to me at the station. I saw her again when I went over to the hotel with Austin. She's been sent down by her husband to keep an eye on the new lot of builders.'

'Was that flashy-looking young man the foreman?'

'The boss.'

'And are his men going to panic, as the last lot did?'

'I doubt it. Mrs Selby hopes they will. She doesn't want to live here. I don't like her, but I feel sorry for her, I don't know why.'

'I know why. You feel sorry because she wants you to feel sorry. I daresay she makes out that she has no control over her husband's actions. That disarms you. If I were you, I'd keep away from her; he's known to be insanely jealous, and that kind of husband doesn't wait for explanations. Did you say she was staying at Cristall's?'

'Yes.'

'Then you must tell Austin not to get involved. She'll probably interest herself in the man I met on the beach this morning when I took the dogs down for a walk. I don't know what his name is, but he told me he was staying at the hotel. Perhaps you saw him—fifties, good-looking and in good condition for a man of his age. He used to judge dogs, he told me. Perhaps he ought to be warned about Mrs Selby's jealous husband.'

'No need.' Oliver took her empty glass and refilled it. 'He's a great reader—buries his nose in a book and doesn't surface until it's time to go to bed.'

'Did this builder show any reluctance to go into the house this morning?'

'Not the slightest. If his men are like him, we've heard the last of ghosts.'

'Perhaps. But something tells me we haven't. There are the others—go and let them in, will you?'

She greeted the guests warmly and dispensed generous portions of sherry or martini, and then led the way to the dining room, where plates were piled on the table, and knives, forks, spoons and glasses laid out in rows.

'You must all help yourselves,' she told them. 'The mayonnaise curdled a bit, as you see, but I think it's far nicer, curdled or not, than the stuff you buy in bottles. There's mustard over there. Oliver, will you take charge of the wine? It's rather good; my brother recommended it. The potato salad looks a little tired, because I can never induce poor old Trotter to cook the potatoes enough, and she usually forgets to put in salt. Jeanne, you'll notice that I remembered how the French like *crudités*, so I prepared some.'

Austin was regarding them with distaste— raw carrots cut into thick slices, raw turnips cut into thin slices, heart of cabbage left whole-leaved, cucumber in small chunks, raw flowerets of cauliflower, and a surrounding of onion rings. He looked hopefully towards the plate from which he had been helped to a single slice of thinly-cut ham. It was empty. The potatoes in the salad were half-cooked. He looked sourly at his hostess's ample curves and thought morosely that this was not what she ate when she was alone. Thick soups, he shouldn't wonder, and stews with dumplings, and puddings oozing cream.

'I've made one of my nice trifles,' Lady Cressing was saying. 'It's the one thing most people find impossible to make a success of. A trifle, I always tell them, is a *creation*. You build it up layer by layer, each layer perfect, so easy if only you—'

'—use your imagination,' put in Austin, and wished he hadn't, as Lady Cressing's ringing laugh made the glasses tinkle.

'Quite right, quite right,' she said. 'And then, to finish it off, one adds one's little secrets.'

The best secret, Austin discovered, cautiously testing a spoonful of a mess of custard, jelly and sponge cake, was the flavouring. Rum. Lots and lots of rum, he noted with pleasure—so much, that he thought there must have been some overlapping, with dear old Trotter unaware that it had already been laced, and emptying the bottle over it. He held out his plate for a second helping, and then, to Lady Cressing's delight, a third. This last portion, taken from the bottom of the dish, proved to be almost pure spirit. Licking the

187

last fumes from his spoon, he felt a warm glow stealing over him. Not much to eat, he thought, but nobody could fault the liquid refreshment. Offered a liqueur with his coffee, he chose instead to top it up with more rum. After this, he felt that he could face with fortitude whatever parlour games they were made to play.

There were no parlour games.

'Now I'll tell you what we're going to do.' Lady Cressing had placed her guests in a circle in the drawing room, and was standing in the centre holding a sheaf of sheet music. 'We're going to sing madrigals.'

There was an instant's stunned silence, and then a chorus of protest, out of which Elva's firm tones rose.

'You must leave me out,' she said. 'I can't sing.'

'Me neither.' Austin with difficulty suppressed a hiccup. 'Count me out.'

'Nonsense, nonsense,' Lady Cressing said indulgently. 'If you can speak, you can sing. One of the reasons I went to London recently was to buy the music. I'm going to start a choir in Rocksea, and we shall sing nothing but madrigals.' She began to hand out the sheets of music. 'We're going to begin with a nice, easy one: "Come, Cuckoo, Come". It's a very well-known one, seventeenth century. Madrigals originated in Italy and were revived in the sixteenth and seventeenth centuries, but I

188

daresay you all know that.'

Nobody knew that.

'But you must have sung madrigals at school!' she protested.

'Never,' Roberta said. 'I would have complained to my parents.'

'Now you mustn't joke,' Lady Cressing reproved. 'It's a pity you're not all going to be here permanently—you could have formed the nucleus of my choir. As you see, the words of this madrigal are beautiful. Madrigals weren't written in Latin, because they weren't for church use; they were written to words in the language of the singers, in this case English. Now we must allocate the parts.'

'I can't read music,' Roberta objected.

'Nonsense, Roberta dear. You all went to expensive schools; they couldn't have neglected your musical education to that extent. You must have sung to music at some time during your schooldays.'

'There was a chart,' Roberta admitted, 'with ta-fe-toffee. I never knew what it was all about.'

'We are not going to do Tonic Sol-fa. Jeanne, will you pay attention?'

'I'm coaching her,' Oliver said. 'She's all at sea. She doesn't speak our musical language.'

'Of course she doesn't. She uses the terms used in Latin countries. Our Soh is her Sol. Our Fah is her Fa. Our note D is her Re. It's perfectly simple. Now stop pretending to be

189

donkeys, all of you, and we'll begin.'

'I really can't sing,' Elva protested. 'I've never sung a note in my life.'

'Until now. If I had my way,' Lady Cressing declared, 'there would be less of these gymnastics and far, far more singing to get air into your lungs and fill your systems with oxygen. Now listen and I'll run through the beginning of "Cuckoo". Have you all got the place? Good. We won't bother with the words yet; just the melody. As you must know, this is contrapuntal and—'

'This is what?' Austin enquired.

'Just think of it as counterpoint, a combination of two or more melodies. Of course there's double and triple counter-point, but we won't go into that now. First I must give you the note.'

She walked to the neglected grand piano and sounded a note. There was a cracked, tremulous response.

'Wants tuning,' Lady Cressing said. 'Mm, mm, mm—that's it.' She opened her mouth and gave voice to the first two lines of the madrigal. The sound was unexpectedly pleasing—a mellow contralto issuing from somewhere behind the massive bosom. There was involuntary applause as she ended.

'Thank you. You see how easy it is? I shall count four in a bar. You begin when I say four. Ready? One, two, three, FOUR. One, two three . . . One moment, one moment. Elva, try

190

it again, my dear. You're singing the same note again and again, and you're an octave too low.'

'I know. All I can do is drone.'

'That's true,' Austin corroborated. 'She used to do the bottom end of bagpipes.'

'She can sing just as well as anybody else if she tries. Jeanne, you have a very true voice; could you make it a little louder?'

'I'll try.'

The second attempt was no better. There was an interval while Elva was given a private rehearsal, which ended in her being able to transfer her one-note performance an octave higher.

'If you'll let me do the high part,' Austin offered, 'I'd do it better. Listen.'

He broke into a pure, only slightly shrill soprano. Lady Cressing, on the point of calling for order, changed her mind. She wanted voices, and here was an obvious leader.

'Well, it's rather unorthodox,' she said, 'but at least it's clear and in tune and it does give some idea of what we're aiming at. Do it again, Austin, but wait until Oliver has recovered; he's being quite idiotic. Ready? One, two, three, FOUR . . .'

It was not singing of a high order and it did not sound like a madrigal, but with the choir mistress passionately urging them, they achieved a certain degree of success, and only when they were walking home realised that they had promised to take part in future sessions.

'I didn't promise anything,' Elva said. 'It was the rest of you. She'd rather I kept my drone away. Austin, will you stop shrilling?'

Austin, uplifted by strong spirits and promotion to choir leader, reluctantly obeyed. They separated at the gate of the cottage, Austin to drive to the hotel, the others to go to bed.

Jeanne, feeling thirsty, went into the kitchen to make herself a drink. Oliver, having taken Trotter back to Lady Cressing's door, joined her.

'Thirsty, like me?' he asked.

'Yes. I'm making coffee. Want some?'

'Yes. Or better still, cocoa. You used to make rather good cocoa; see if you've forgotten how.'

'Water, milk, or half and half?'

'Milk, if I'm not robbing your children. There's chocolate powder in one of those cupboards, if you girls haven't found it and used it all, as you did the wine.'

She found it and measured some into a cup. He sat watching her.

'Enjoy the evening?' he asked.

'Yes. Don't you feel sorry for Boris now that your mother and David have gone?'

'I suppose I do. She used to see a lot of them. But she's got a lot of friends all over the town—she's not lonely.'

'That isn't quite the same as having nice

192

neighbours. I'm glad she's got Trotter to look after her.' She gave him his cup of chocolate. 'More sugar?'

'No, thanks. Where are those fancy biscuits the twins were eating?'

'Hidden away. Roberta likes them. You can't have any; they're fattening.'

She was seated opposite to him, pouring out her coffee. When she put down the coffee pot, he reached across the table and took one of her hands and let it lie on his outstretched one.

'Look at that,' he said. 'I could almost close my fist with your hand inside it. Like this. You're really pint-sized, aren't you?'

'My father said I fitted nicely into my clothes.'

He released her hand.

'Do you ever worry about the future?' he asked.

She considered, sipping coffee.

'Worry? No. Not now. I used to worry when I first realised that I wasn't in love with Paul. I was frightened sometimes when I thought of two babies, myself, and nobody else. And I used to worry most because I couldn't make my marriage work.'

He said nothing. He was looking at the hand he had held in his, and wondering how Paul Brisson could have let it slip out of his grasp. Then he put a question.

'When Elva and Roberta leave, why don't you stay on?' he asked.

193

Her eyes widened.

'Here? In this cottage?'

'Why not? Is there any hurry to get to France?'

'There is no hurry. But the sooner I make a new life—'

'You're not ready to make a new life. You've been unwinding ever since you came here. Every time I see you, you're more like the old Jeanne. The young Jeanne. There's no problem yet about school for the twins. If you want to send them to a nursery school, there are two good ones in Rocksea. Would you mind being here with the prospect of having Maurice Selby and his wife as neighbours?'

'No. But—'

'If you're going to point out that the rent for you alone should be less than the rent for the three of you, I'll make a generous gesture and reduce it. On condition, of course, that I still have the use of my room. Once Elva and Roberta go, there'll be room for Austin. You can then make me a proposition: that you run the house for the two of us and pay no rent at all. Short of giving you the cottage, what more can I do?'

She was staring at him in an attempt to guess how much of this was meant seriously. His expression looked merely business-like.

'It's very nice of you to have thought of it,' she said slowly, 'but—'

'But no?'

'I didn't say no.'

'If you didn't, it means you're thinking it over. I don't want to rush you into anything. I know very well that this cottage has many drawbacks, and you might feel that you couldn't be comfortable in it for—'

'I *love* this cottage!' she broke in passionately. 'I *love* it. There is nowhere else I could have stayed and been so happy as I am now, nowhere! To be here, to work in this kitchen, to have the beach so close, the shops too, to feel myself really at home—where else could I have felt this? But—'

'There are always Buts. They crop up and do their best to spoil things—but why not live for a while with that picture you've just painted? Don't plan, don't look ahead, or not too far ahead. The advice I've given you, the plan I've suggested, is the one my mother would have put to you if she'd been alive. She would have—my God, have I said something?'

She was weeping. She had pushed aside her cup and put her head on her arms and was giving way to unrestrained tears. He watched her in dismay.

'It's the coffee,' he diagnosed at last. 'Not a good thing last thing at night. You should have had some nice hot chocolate to build you up, like me. Have you got a hanky?'

She produced one, raised her head and wiped the tears from her cheeks.

'Feel better?' he asked.

'Yes.'

'Would it be too much to ask what set you off?'

'I don't know. Relief, I think. Gratitude, maybe.'

'Gratitude? For the offer of a housekeeper's job?'

'No. I was grateful for the excuse to put off deciding what I want to do with my life. Because whatever I thought of doing was never so nice as what I'm doing now.'

'Didn't you consider staying on?'

'No. I thought of this as a ... a sort of interlude with Elva and Roberta. When they went, it seemed natural that I should go too. I never thought of it as anything but a stop-over. That may seem silly, but it's true. You think I would make a good housekeeper?'

'You'll certainly make a good cook. Are you going to take the job?'

'Yes.'

He laid his hand on the table, palm uppermost. She put her own on it.

'A bargain,' he said. 'Signed this night by Big Mitt and Small Paw, in the presence of a friendly ghost. In the ... You're not going to howl again, are you?'

'No.'

'I'm not sure. The weather report says there's more rain on the way.' He rose, came round the table and pulled her to her feet. 'May I see you to your room, Madame

196

Brisson?'

She paused to clear away the cups, and he took them from her and put them back on the table.

'First down to breakfast clears away,' he said.

'But I'm nearly always first.'

'All the more reason for leaving them. Bedtime.' He walked with her to her room. 'Do you ever feel lonely in bed?' he asked.

She gave a shaky laugh.

'Sometimes, yes.'

He opened the door.

'That,' he said, 'is the next problem we shall have to tackle.'

He closed the door after her, stood looking at it for some moments, and then switched off the lights and went up to his room.

CHAPTER SEVEN

Neither Oliver nor Austin was seen at the cottage during the following week. Oliver was in London, Austin in Yorkshire. The reactions of the three women in their absence varied: Elva hoped they would stay away, Roberta missed them in the evenings and Jeanne, to her dismay, made the discovery that Oliver leaving the kitchen untidy, Oliver bringing in sand on his feet and spreading it over the

197

floors, Oliver keeping the twins awake by playing games with them, was infinitely preferable to no Oliver at all.

As he had told her, Elva was not stimulating company. She thought that only loyalty must have prevented him from going farther and labelling her dull. But she was restful, more reliable than Roberta, and undemanding. She rose early, went down to the beach before the others were up, had a swim and then came back to the cottage and made herself some coffee. She stayed in her room working until lunch time, but did not join the others for a picnic meal; she ate by herself in the kitchen. She came down punctually to dinner, hungry and ready to enjoy the meal.

The scene before dinner was not as lively as it had been when the men were present. While Jeanne made the final preparations, Roberta sat watching her and talking, cigarette in one hand, drink in the other. She talked whether the other two listened or not. Elva gave her a small part of her mind, the rest being bent on chess problems, the board and the pieces spread on a small table in front of her. As a change from chess problems she amused herself by getting meteorological information from the telephone and drawing up complicated weather charts, exasperating Roberta, who could see no future for a girl who spent her time on anti-cyclones.

The work of redecorating Parson's House

had progressed speedily and without incident, but soon after it began, Lady Cressing and the occupants of the cottage found themselves in the unlooked-for position of hoping that the Selbys would come into residence as soon as possible. For unwelcome as they would be, their arrival would mean the departure of the Dents. Dot and Reg, daily sunning themselves on the terrace, had been joined by the elder Dent and his wife, known to all within earshot as Mum and Dad. While the workmen, a stolid group, went on with the work, Dad shouted over the hammering, his wife spread picnic lunches, Reg played jazz loudly on cassettes and Dot, enlivened by the music, broke into song and dance. Nobody, moaned Lady Cressing, stopping at the cottage on her way down to the beach with the dogs, nobody objected to seeing people happy, but couldn't they be happy more quietly?

For the past fifteen years, the occupants of Parson's House, Vistamar and the cottage had avoided putting up any kind of screen between the houses. They were friends, neighbours, coming and going freely from one to another, not at all disturbed by the fact that their side windows were in clear view. Now it was a matter for regret; when Maurice Selby came into residence, he would undoubtedly make arrangements for greater privacy, but for the moment, it was impossible to avoid the sight as well as the sound of the Dents. So far, they had not invaded the little beach, but Lady Cressing felt that this was only a matter of time. Jeanne tried to imagine settling down on the sand with the twins with the Dents a few yards away, and agreed with Roberta that this would be the end of their pleasant picnics.

They received one evening an unexpected and unwelcome visitor. There was a knock on the front door, followed a few moments later by a loud tattoo on the door of the kitchen. Opening it, Jeanne saw on the doorstep a young man, hatless, in a light grey suit with a mackintosh over his shoulder.

'Press,' he said. 'Good evening.'

He gave her a smile which was intended to be friendly but which had in it so much excess of self-confidence that she felt he was using it professionally. She was wondering whether it was necessary to ask him in, when she found him walking past her, through the arch and into the sitting room. Roberta, pouring herself out a drink, looked at him and then past him, enquiringly, to Jeanne.

'Press,' he said again, and dropped his mackintosh on a chair. 'The name's Priest. Mike Priest. Hine *Gazette*. Sorry to bother you girls at this hour, but it's pure chance, and not design, that made me choose the very moment you'd be knocking it back. Now this'—he took a step forward and picked up a bottle—'is something that soared out of my price range years ago. Do I help myself, or do I wait to be asked?'

'You wait to be asked,' Roberta said frostily, 'and in this case you don't get asked because it isn't my whisky.'

'Where's the owner?'

'Away.'

'Thank God. She—he?—won't begrudge me a snort, will he, she?'

He had picked up a glass and was pouring whisky into it. So swiftly had he moved that short of wresting the bottle from his grasp, there was nothing Roberta could do but watch.

Elva, coming down to dinner, heard voices, frowned, turned and walked upstairs again. Mr Priest, after going to the tap in the kitchen to add water to his whisky, returned to the sitting room, took a chair and sat smiling at the two women, who were standing regarding him with open dislike.

'Your health.' He raised his glass. 'And the owner's, God bless him or her. Don't begrudge me this small reward for my labours, ladies; I've earned it. I've been out all day on this job, and got nowhere.'

'Except to the whisky,' Roberta said.

'As you say.' He held the drink up to the light and looked at it with affection. 'Lovely stuff, really lovely.' His glance went to the women. 'I'll tell you something. I used to have nice manners, once. Well brought up. Take your hat off when you pass a lady, never say a nasty swear word, always carry a lady's parcels and never let a lady down. The kids in the street knocked it out of me before I was eight, but some remnants stuck. When I took a job as travelling salesman, I couldn't put my foot in the door. Not at first. Nasty thing to do, I thought, shoving your dirty great boot into the door so's the busy housewife couldn't shut it and get back to the telly. Then I discovered that manners might make the man, but they don't make a success of the job. If you don't push, you get pushed; it's as simple as that. And if a travelling salesman needs armour plating, how much more does a reporter?'

'People—some people—are only too glad of a chance to talk to the Press,' Roberta told him.

'Right. Perfectly, perfectly right.' He drained his glass, gazed into it and then held it out to her in appeal. 'Have a heart,' he begged.

She glanced at Jeanne. Jeanne gave a slight nod, and Roberta took the glass and, in Mr Priest's words, repeated the dose.

'For that,' he said as he took it from her, 'you'll sing with the angels in Heaven. If they sing. I often wonder. The sort that get to Heaven never seem to me to be the singing sort. What were we saying? Oh yes, people talking to reporters. They do, as you say— some of them. Publicity hunters. People dying to see their name in print, even if it's only as winners of the local Bingo competition. People who saw an accident and want to tell you what they thought they saw. But when a reporter goes out after information and looks for it among—shall we call them?—normal people, all he draws is a blank.' He put his glass on the table and leaned forward. 'Take this ghost business. Workmen, firm of Quinter, put on the job. They see spooks and give in their notice. The head of the firm loses the contract. So the reporter thinks it's a sensible idea to have a chat with this Quinter, to ask him what gives. What does Quinter do? Says the men didn't feel well, and knocked off work. His wife says the same, in exactly the same words. The reporter looks up the workmen and hopes they're the type that want to see their name in print. They're not. They're thinking of future jobs and don't want to handicap themselves by getting known as the chaps who saw ghosts, or snakes, or pink elephants. They want to forget the whole thing. The only one who's willing to talk is an old cleaning woman, and she's been telling the story for so long that it's mushroomed into a saga, losing authenticity as it grew.'

'I thought the whole idea of being a reporter,' Roberta said, 'was to be able to spin a story out of threads.'

'I've never heard it put that way. But you're wrong. It's not threads he needs; it's bones. He can put on the trimming, but he needs one or two solid facts to build on. I haven't even got half a one. Nobody on any paper this side of

Exeter has scraped up enough to write a story with. All that's been printed so far is speculation.'

'That's all it is—speculation,' Jeanne said. 'What else is any story about ghosts? What facts are there about ghosts?'

'Well, one fact,' said Mr Priest, 'is what they look like. The baffling bit of this assignment is that nobody seems to have seen anything. The first thing people tell you when they claim to have seen a ghost is what the thing looked like. Headless. Got a sword sticking out of it. Dagger in the chest. Long white nightgown. Dressed in fifteenth-century attire, but transparent. Dragging a long chain. Those are what I call bones. But this I-felt-a-push angle doesn't get me anywhere. Isn't there anybody who can put me on to someone who *saw* anything?'

'No,' said Jeanne.

'No,' said Roberta.

'You both spent school holidays in that house—right?'

'Yes,' said Roberta.

'And you've been into it recently, right?'

'Yes. Five of us went in, and nothing happened. Nothing at all.'

'Quinter said his partner fell off a ladder. Were you there?'

'We'd just left,' Roberta said. 'Is this going to be printed?'

'Why not? You must be used to publicity.

You're the creator of Sideways. Yes, this is going to be printed. I can't get photographs of your friends, but I can get plenty of you, and I'll use a good one.'

'And quote me?'

'Fully. So now you ring for the butler to heave me out. Before you do that, could you remember that reporters have to make a living, and they do it for the most part without any help from the general public. If we didn't wrest a story out of unwilling talkers, we'd soon be what they nowadays call redundant, which means out on our ears. As one writer to another: are you holding out on me?'

'No. The people you ought to talk to,' Roberta said, 'are the Dents. The firm of Dent took over from the firm of Quinter and there hasn't been a ghost heard of—or felt—since.'

'I tried that line. All I got was a history of the Dent firm, related by the son. So—' He paused and wrinkled his nose and sniffed. 'Roast beef?'

'Veal,' Jeanne corrected. 'But enough for three only.'

'One—two—am I number three?'

'No, you're not,' said Roberta. 'Number three's lurking upstairs, longing for her dinner and praying for you to go away. If I give you another whisky that doesn't belong to me, and if we both swear we can't tell you anything about ghosts, and if I tell you you can write what you like about me, with photographs, will you return to your desk at the Hine *Gazette*?'

'Without anything to eat?'

Roberta, once again, looked at Jeanne. This time Jeanne shook her head. Mr Priest rose, took the glass Roberta handed him, and raised it to utter a toast.

'To your children,' he said. 'May they all be reporters.'

He drained the glass, picked up his mackintosh, nodded, and followed Jeanne to the door. He did not look back.

'I wouldn't give him dinner,' Jeanne said, 'because he was sure we were going to.'

Elva, coming downstairs, took her place at the table and was told the story of the visit.

'I couldn't help feeling sorry for him,' Roberta ended.

'Sorry for him . . . no,' said Jeanne. 'I don't like it when people use charm as he did.'

'Everybody uses charm, if they've got it,' Elva remarked.

'If they use it, they haven't got it,' Jeanne said with so much conviction that her hearers found nothing to say.

The delay had made them enjoy the food even more than usual.

'I hope I don't put on weight,' Roberta said anxiously. 'Why can't we all be like Austin, who eats like a horse and never puts on an ounce?'

'Trotter eats well, too,' Jeanne said. 'I left her a lot of sandwiches—more than I thought she could eat. But there wasn't one left.'

'No. I forgot to tell you,' Roberta said. 'She shared them with the twins.'

'With the twins?' Jeanne spoke incredulously. 'The twins were in bed. They were in bed before Trotter came to baby-sit.'

'But when she went in to take their books away and turn out the lights, she decided it wouldn't do them any harm to share her supper.'

'How do you know?'

'By listening to the twins. Jo likes crab sandwiches but Polly prefers pâté.'

'Do you mean that she gave them—'

'Why not?' Elva asked reasonably. 'You made them yourself; you know they're good.'

'But to feed the children . . . that's not baby-sitting.'

'It's one kind,' Elva said. 'Some let the children sit up and watch television. What does it matter? Their function is to prevent the children from setting the house on fire or falling over high balconies. If your children are well and happy when you come home, what more can you ask?'

'I agree,' Roberta said. 'You can't have baby-sitters to do anything but sit. I don't suppose—'

She was interrupted by a sudden movement from Duke. The next moment, he rushed to the door and stood tense and quivering. They had not switched on the light; the room was

207

suddenly illuminated by the headlights of a car. Duke's excited barking told them who had arrived.

Oliver paused in the doorway to study the scene.

'Picturesque,' he commented. 'What are you still sitting over dinner for?'

'We started late. We had a visitor,' Jeanne said. 'Where's Austin?'

'Still up in Leeds. He'll be back in a day or two—he wants to have his birthday here. Who was your visitor?'

'Hine *Gazette*,' Roberta said. 'I'm going to appear, photograph and interview.'

Oliver frowned.

'I hope you didn't talk too much,' he said. 'There was an account in two of the Exeter papers today. We don't want any more swarms of people coming to—My God, you gave him my whisky!'

'It was there, in full view,' Roberta said apologetically.

'It was there, in full bottle. Look at it now. Did you let him help himself?'

'Only the first time. After that I doled it out.'

'Generously, I can see. Why don't I lock up my drink?'

'You can if you want to,' Jeanne told him. 'Do you want some coffee?'

'Yes. I'll make some.'

'No. I will.'

'He's not gifted,' Roberta said, 'but he is capable of making coffee for himself.'

'I know that,' Jeanne answered. 'But I hate seeing men doing domestic things. They look so silly.'

'Why do they look sillier in a kitchen than anywhere else?' Elva wanted to know.

'I don't know why—but they do. So much muscle, so much force wasted on light work. Let them go and dig in the garden, or put up curtains or put down carpets. Unless they are chefs, let them keep out of the kitchen. At least, out of my kitchen when I have one.'

'Won't you dress your next husband in a fancy apron with *Sexy Soapsuds* on it?' Oliver asked her.

'No, I will not.'

'Then post me an application form. How's the work going next door?'

They told him. In chorus, and then individually, they reported in full on the Dent family. Listening, he frowned.

'Sounds like a fairground,' he commented. 'But I don't understand—hasn't Mrs Selby visited the house at all?'

'I've never seen her there,' Roberta answered. 'And they must know she's not coming, or why would they carry out easy chairs and spread your mother's Mexican rugs on the terrace?'

'It's much worse than a fairground,' Elva said. 'You can get away from a fairground.

Can't you say something to Mrs Selby?'

'No need,' Oliver said. 'He's arriving soon.'

'How do you know?' Jeanne asked.

'I got a letter from him. Four lines. He wants me to go up to the house when he arrives and look at a few pieces of furniture. He didn't say what they were, but I know: they're things that David bought for my mother.'

'Is he going to give them to you?' Roberta asked.

'Give? No. He's going to sell them, but he's giving me the chance of buying. Which I'm going to do. I didn't want her to leave the things in the house, but she was determined not to give Maurice Selby any chance of saying she took what didn't belong to her. Have the Dents been down to the beach?'

'So far, no,' Roberta said.

'And no talk of ghosts?'

'None,' Elva said. 'But when the scare dies down, the legend will persist.'

'I daresay. How are the twins?'

'They're fine,' Jeanne said. 'Did you teach them to throw dog biscuits to Duke?'

'The idea was to teach Duke how to catch them, but it turned into a lesson in how to throw. I shouldn't leave them alone with the dog biscuits. They like them.'

'They . . . they *ate* them?'

'Like lollipops.'

'So there you are,' Roberta told Jeanne.

210

'You don't have to worry—they've proved what wonderful digestions they've got. Crab, pâté and dog biscuits.' She gave a long yawn. 'So there's no need to fuss.'

Waking next morning, Jeanne found that there was nobody to fuss over—the twins were not in the room. She went into the kitchen; there was nobody there, but she saw evidence that the twins had eaten under the supervision of an adult. The table had been cleared. As she could not see the beach from the window, she walked outside, looked down and saw both children in the water with Oliver.

She joined them when she had had breakfast, and found them eating apples.

'Good morning. Fruit first thing in the morning, very health-giving,' Oliver said.

She spread her towel and sat beside him.

'Third thing,' she corrected. 'Breakfast, one. Swim, two. Apple, three. I suppose the twins heard you in the kitchen, and joined you?'

He shook his head and finished his mouthful of apple.

'Wrong. I heard them. I put my ear to your door and heard murmurs, so I went in and got them out of their cots and fed them. They dressed themselves while I got breakfast ready. I would have taken you in some, but I could see you were going to sleep for at least another hour. Do you always curl up like that in bed?'

'I don't know. You must be a very quiet mover.'

211

'You must be a very heavy sleeper. It makes me wonder what'll happen if someone tries to burgle my house. A lot of protection you're going to be. Want to come with me to see Mr Quinter?'

'Yes. Did you see they've started on the wall?'

'Yes. What's the difference? We won't want to go up there when Maurice Selby and his wife move in. All the same, it feels like the end of an era.' He paused. 'Oddly enough, I can't imagine Mrs Selby living there. She was banking on getting out of it if the house was haunted, but as it isn't, she'll have to think of something else—and that's what I think she'll do: find some other means of escape. But that's her problem. How about you? Have you given any part of your mind to the proposition I made last week about your future?'

'Yes.'

'You're staying on?'

'Yes. For a time. I'll be very happy here, and so will the twins.'

'Good. I've been giving my mind to the matter, too, and I've come to the conclusion that if you ever take the decision to leave this country, where you have friends, associations, ties of a kind, and go to France, to people you don't know and for whom you've no affection—and what's more, of whom you have no knowledge more recent than your childhood—I'm going to do what I can to stop

212

you.'

'But—'

'Try listening for a change. How do you know that you're not going to prove a super-efficient housekeeper? How do you know I won't ask you to stay for ever? If I asked you, at this moment, to stay for ever, you'd refuse. You might even panic. So I'm going to exercise patience. And now you can talk if you want to.'

She said nothing. She was studying his expression, but she could read nothing in it but a calm, business-like look that matched the words he had just spoken.

'No comment?' he asked.

'There's nothing to say. Except thank you.'

'Then that's that. And now we'll go and call on Mr Quinter, and take the twins with us. And on the way back, we'll drop into Cristall's and make arrangements for Austin's birthday dinner. Let's go.'

Mr Quinter was not at home; he was at work on a building site about a mile away from his house. While the twins found their way to the piles of bricks and sand, he led Jeanne and Oliver to a platform of planks and invited them to be seated.

'I'm not going to ask you to tell me 'ow the work's going on at Parson's 'ouse,' he said. 'I know 'ow it's going. People come and tell me. Some of them say I was made a laughing-stock, and some of them say they don't believe it was a false alarm. I don't think it was, either, but facts are facts, and there's those men of Dents not showing a sign of trouble. I'm so confused, I don't know what to think.'

'Neither do I,' Oliver said. 'Trying to figure it out is what Mr David Selby used to call unprofitable speculation. What I came for was to say that when you're not feeling so confused, you'll remember that a good deal of the building work in this town comes through Mr Parkes, and he has asked me to tell you that if you want the job of building the Parkes block, it's yours. We'll try and arrange that the work goes through without the same trouble as the last, but whether it does or not, you'll be in charge.'

There was silence. Mr Quinter nodded several times, made some growling noises in his throat and at last put out a hand and solemnly shook Oliver's.

'I won't say thank you, Mr Hobart. I don't know 'ow to. Tell Mr Parkes I'll do the best I can for 'im.'

'I will.'

They collected the twins and drove away.

'Next stop, Cristall's,' Oliver said. 'When we've fixed up Austin's affair, we'll see if Mrs Selby's around. I'd like you to meet her.'

When they asked for her, they were told that she was in her room; told that Mr Hobart would like to see her, she said that she would come down.

They waited for her in the bar adjoining the

214

entrance hall, and when she came in, Oliver thought that she was looking several years older than she had done at Exeter station. She made no attempt at a greeting.

'Let's drink,' she said. 'No, not that table; this one. It's darker. I'm not looking my best.'

'This is Madame Brisson, one of my tenants.'

'Scotch on the rocks for me. How about you and your tenant?'

'We can't stay. Her children are in the car.'

'Then get them out and I'll send someone to keep them amused. What age?'

'Twins of four,' Jeanne said.

'Carlos'—Mrs Selby addressed the barman—'twins of four in a car outside. Send someone to keep an eye on them, will you? But serve these drinks first. Do they like nuts or crisps or olives or anything of that sort?' she asked Jeanne.

'They'd like an ice, if you—'

'Strawberry ices for the twins, Carlos.' She took her drink from the tray he brought, and leaned back to study Oliver. 'This is the second time you've walked in here just when I needed you,' she told him. 'I was upstairs trying to decide between sleeping pills and hurling myself through the window.'

'You haven't been up to Parson's House.'

'No. Not since I went up that first day with you, and met that ape, Dent. He's been down here every day, reporting, and he's sent written reports to Maurice. No ghosts. Not a sign of one. So I'm lost. But'—she drained her glass and signalled to the barman for a refill—'get this, Hobart. I-am-not-going-to-live-here. You heard me?'

'I heard you.'

'I heard you too,' Jeanne said, 'and I find it strange, because I would give anything to be able to live here always.'

'Then you can have it. You can have it all— this morgue of a hotel, this town, the view if any, the air—and Parson's House. Take the lot.' Her eyes went to Oliver. 'Has Maurice written to you about the furniture?'

'Yes.'

'If he wasn't the jealous devil he is, he'd have asked me to give you a message. And if he wasn't the miserly devil he is, he would have given you the things. They're not his; David paid for them. I suppose you'll buy them?'

'Yes.'

'I thought you would. Will you order drinks? Your glass is empty.'

'I'm sorry.' He looked at Jeanne, and they rose. 'We've got to go.'

She said nothing; she sat motionless, staring into her glass.

The twins were on a swing in the garden in charge of a doorman. They put them into the car and drove back to the cottage.

'Not a happy woman,' Jeanne commented on the way.

'No. I'd go further and say she was a desperate woman.'

'Desperate simply because she doesn't want to live here?'

'That—and something else, if I'm not mistaken. She must be lining up alternatives.'

Jeanne said nothing. In her mind was relief and deep thankfulness. She herself need not seek alternatives. She had chosen.

CHAPTER EIGHT

Austin's birthday celebration, held for the past few years at Cristall's Restaurant, was rather more than a family-and-friends affair; it embraced, in greater or lesser degree, the chef, the *maître d'hôtel*, the waiters and the kitchen staff as well as chambermaids and the dignified gentlemen who presided at the reception desk. Thus diners at the restaurant on the night of the party found the service for once less than perfect, since the waiters devoted most of their attention to a table in the corner by the widest window, laid for six.

Lady Cressing was, as always, a member of the party. Trotter was baby-sitting at the cottage. A birthday dinner had been sent over from the restaurant, and they left her sitting down to enjoy it. How much of it would find its way to the twins, Jeanne did not care to speculate.

They gathered in the residents' bar, which was never very well patronised; tonight they had it to themselves. Lady Cressing was in very good spirits, and over a sherry, divulged the reason for her satisfaction.

'I've brought it off at last,' she announced triumphantly. 'I've won. They've given in. We're going to get it.'

'Get what?' Roberta asked.

'Transport. I was determined to get a bus, and I've got a bus. Only a small one, but it's going to run twice a day in each direction—Belling to Rocksea, Rocksea back to Belling.'

'Where's Belling?' Jeanne asked.

'It's the new group of houses they built about four miles from Rocksea—not the Hine side, the other side,' Lady Cressing explained. 'Houses for the retired and the elderly, but no means of getting anywhere. Now at last I've convinced the authorities that the poor old pensioners must have a bus. I can't *tell* you what a difference it's going to make to poor old Trotter.'

'What's it got to do with Trotter?' Austin asked, puzzled.

'My dear boy, don't you see? The bus will have to stop at the intersection, and the intersection is just at the end of our promontory road, so now all Trotter has to do is wait until the bus stops, and get on to it and she'll be at the shops in no time. And so will I,

218

when necessary. No longer will I have to risk being blown to my death off that overhead bridge when there's a gale blowing. But it would have been no use hoping that any transport would be provided for Trotter or for me. Now the Belling people have got it and we shall be, so to speak, subsidiary beneficiaries. Shall we drink a toast to Austin?

'I want to remind you all,' she said when it was drunk, 'that my Madrigal Club is having its first rehearsal on Sunday. It has to be Sunday because so many of them aren't free during the week. We're going to rehearse at Vistamar from half past three to half past four, and then I shall give them all tea. I shall expect you all to be there.'

Oliver, putting his glass on the table, signalled to Austin and by a slight gesture brought his attention to a solitary figure seated on a divan in the hall.

'She looks lonely,' Austin said in an undertone. 'But will she mix?'

'It's your decision. This is your party.'

'I shan't enjoy it much if I have to look at her stuck at a table by herself. She's used to dining alone, but she might like to be asked to join us. Will you ask her, or shall I?'

'You're the host. Boris won't like it.'

'If they're coming to live at Parson's House, she's got to run into them some time, hasn't she?' He leaned forward and addressed Lady Cressing. 'In a corner of the hall,' he told her,

219

'there's a lonely outcast.'

'I know that. I've got good eyesight,' she said. 'I suppose you're proposing to ask her to join the party?'

'Would you enjoy your dinner, seeing her left out?'

'Very much more than I will if she's brought in. But it's a kind thought and it's your party. I just want to be reassured that next time I pass her in the town, I can pretend I've left my glasses at home.'

They watched as Austin went out of the bar and spoke to Mrs Selby. After a moment she rose, picked up her drink and walked with him to join the others. Oliver brought another chair into the circle, and Austin performed the introductions.

'This is Mrs Selby, sister-in-law of David. This is Lady Cressing, who will be a next-door neighbour. Madame Brisson, from Canada—you've already met her. Roberta Murray, creator of Sideways the Crab. And in the chair next to you, Elva Royce, which makes five of us who used to come to Parson's House for school holidays.' He indicated the chair Oliver had placed for her. 'Please sit down.'

But Mrs Selby shook her head. Her eyes left Austin and went to Oliver, who noted uneasily her glassy stare and felt that it would have been better to leave her out of the party. Then she spoke in an abrupt, rather breathless tone.

220

'Look, will you forgive me if I don't join you after all? I don't feel too good.'

Austin looked at her anxiously; she looked deathly pale.

'Anything I can get you?' he asked.

'No. I'll be all right. I'm going up to my room.' She gave a brief glance round the circle. 'Sorry, and so on.'

'I'll see you to the lift,' Oliver said.

'You needn't. I'm not going to pass out. Not until I get upstairs, anyhow.'

He said nothing, but accompanied her to the lift. As they approached it, it came down from the floor above and out of it stepped the man Oliver thought of as the book lover. Something about Mrs Selby's pallor kept his eyes on her face, but she turned away and addressed Oliver.

'I'll walk up. It's only one floor. Good night. Sorry about the party.'

Oliver watched her until she disappeared round the bend of the staircase. Then his eyes met those of the other man, who had also been watching her.

'The lady felt ill,' he said.

'Ah.'

They were walking in the direction of the bar. At sight of the large circle gathered round one of the tables, the man hesitated.

'It's all right.' Oliver spoke reassuringly. 'We appear to fill the place, but there's still room. And we're just going in to dinner.'

221

Somewhat reluctantly, it seemed to him, the man preceded him into the bar. He was walking past the members of the party, who had resumed their animated conversation, when there was an exclamation of astonishment from Elva. She rose slowly to her feet and the man turned to face her. There was a sudden silence, and then Elva spoke.

'Hello, Father.'

'Elva!'

For some moments, he seemed unable to say more. His face had become very pale.

'I thought you were in South America,' he said at last. 'I saw a picture of you in—'

'Inaccurate reporting,' she said.

Austin was the first to recover.

'I ordered an extra place,' he told Mr Royce. 'It just got emptied, so you will join us, won't you?'

'Oh . . . thanks. Yes, I'd be very glad to.'

He did not sound pleased, and he looked even less so. It was not possible to guess what Elva was thinking. But Lady Cressing, having taken in the situation, gave voice to what was clearly disapproval.

'When we met on the beach, Mr Royce, you didn't mention that your daughter had been in Rocksea. Didn't you think of calling at the cottage?'

'I thought that Elva—'

'—was in South America. Quite. But she spent some happy years in the house next door

222

to the cottage, and I would have thought you would—'

'I saw it from the beach.'

'You can't see it all from the beach. Are you down here on business?'

'No. As a matter of fact, yes. I heard there was some land for sale, so I thought I'd take a look.'

'Then Elva, you must take your father to see that nice site on the other side of the river. You must make him buy it and build you a nice house on it.'

'I've got a room in London,' Elva pointed out, 'and I can come down to the cottage any time I want to.'

Oliver felt sorry for Austin; this was not the kind of party he had envisaged. Nor did it improve as the evening went on. All the usual birthday ceremonies took place and a large birthday cake was carried in at the end of dinner, but the unity of the party had vanished. Elva made no attempt to engage her father in conversation, and Mr Royce appeared to be sunk in gloom. All Austin's attempts to inject life into the gathering were unavailing.

Walking with Oliver to get the cars at the end of the evening, he voiced his disappointment.

'The thing never got off the ground,' he complained. 'You can't do much with two heavyweights like Elva and her father. He sat there looking as though he'd rather have been

223

anywhere else.'

'I suppose it was bad luck, finding himself in the middle of people who all knew what a rotten parent he is.'

'He could have made an effort. One thing struck me: that if Elva had been a man, she would have been good-looking. There's a strong likeness to her father.'

'What struck me was the fact that if she did live with him, she wouldn't be much use at entertaining his guests. She made even less effort than he did.'

When Lady Cressing had been seen to her door, and Trotter escorted back to Vistamar, the four residents of the cottage sat with Austin in the kitchen and discussed the party.

'Did you find out how long your father's staying?' Roberta asked Elva.

'No.'

'Didn't you ask any questions? Why has he decided to look at land here?'

'He hasn't.' Elva, slouched in her chair, spoke broodingly. 'He said so, but I don't believe it. I always know when he's lying. So did my mother. So as he didn't come to look at land, what's he doing here?'

'Reading,' Austin said. 'He's a great reader.'

Elva stared at him.

'Reader? My father?' she asked in astonishment.

'Yes. Why the surprise? Didn't you know he could read?'

'I've never seen him open a book in my whole life.'

'Well, I saw him with his nose buried in a book, and so did Oliver. He might be trying it to see if he likes it.'

'He asked you to have dinner with him tomorrow, and you said you would,' Roberta remarked. 'Can't you get some information out of him while his mind's on his food?'

'I can try.' She moved restlessly in her chair. 'My mother could have found out what he's here for. She never listened to what he said, only to the way he said it. But I haven't seen enough of him to get any practice at it. Anybody going to make coffee?'

'Not coffee,' Austin said. 'We're going to have my father's favourite party-chaser: black velvet. Stout and champagne. I'll see to the champagne, Oliver, if you'll open the stout. Then we'll all sleep like logs and feel fine in the morning.'

But Oliver felt less than fine when he answered the telephone on the following morning, and heard Maurice Selby's voice.

'Hobart?'

'Yes.'

'Selby here. I'm at Cristall's. You got my letter?'

'Yes.'

'Do you want to see that furniture before I put it up for sale?'

'Yes.'

225

'I'm busy all this afternoon, but I could meet you at the house about six-thirty this evening. Would that suit you?'

'Yes.'

That was all. Oliver glanced at his watch: close on midday. He must have caught a very early train. Perhaps it was not mixing her drinks that had made Mrs Selby look so sick; perhaps he had telephoned to tell her he was arriving in the morning.

He was lunching with a client in Exeter; he worked during the afternoon and returned to the cottage just before six. He had a shower and changed into a suit—he did not feel that this was an occasion for informal attire.

He walked up to the house by the short path—perhaps the last time, he thought, that he would ever use it. There was nobody on the terrace when he reached it, but he heard voices, and in a few moments saw Mrs Selby coming round the side of the house. With her was her husband.

Oliver had not seen him since his boyhood. His first impression was that he had shrunk— and then he remembered his own change in height. He was now taller by a head than the older man. The same hard mouth, he noted; the same cold gaze, the same lurking sneer.

Their greeting was curt, and there was no offer of a handshake.

'We'll go inside and look at the things,' Maurice said. 'I've made a list, with a copy for

226

you.' He handed Oliver a sheet of paper and then turned towards the house. His wife preceded the men through the door, and then stood in the hall.

'This shouldn't take long,' Maurice Selby said. 'You remember the items, of course?'

'Yes.'

'Then we'll look at them and you can mark the ones you want. Drawing room first.'

He drew the dust sheet off a delicate walnut writing desk, the desk at which Lorna Selby had written her letters and done her accounts. Oliver said only three words.

'I'll buy it.'

He bought the gate-legged table in the study and the corner cupboard in the dining room. There remained only the bedroom chair. He followed Maurice Selby up the stairs. Mrs Selby had not moved; she was still standing in the hall.

The chair was by the window in Lorna's room. She had sat in it to read—to herself or to the children. Beside it her husband had placed a low standard lamp. How many times had he sat on the soft, rose-coloured carpet, Oliver wondered, listening to that low, quiet, beautiful voice? It seemed impossible to believe that she would never sit here again, never smile down at them as she closed the book and told them that it was time to get ready for bed . . .

'You'll take it?' he heard Maurice Selby ask.

227

He nodded. They turned and went out of the room and on to the darkened gallery.

Halfway down the stairs, Maurice Selby stopped, felt in his pockets and then said that he had left his copy of the list on the dressing table. Oliver left him to go back for it, and walked slowly down to join Mrs Selby in the hall.

'We're leaving tomorrow,' she told him. Her voice was expressionless. 'He wants me to go with him.'

'There's no more need to watch the workmen?'

'No. The scare's over.'

A bitter note had crept into her voice. She said no more; Maurice Selby was approaching the head of the staircase.

The paper was in his hand. He came down the first three steps, and then stopped, as he had stopped earlier. But this time, he did not feel in his pockets. There was a puzzled expression on his face as he stood staring down at the two in the hall. They saw it change to apprehension. Then he turned his head and looked behind him, and when they saw his face again, it wore a look of terror that made Oliver's mouth go dry. The hand that held the paper went out in a frenzied attempt to grip the banister. It missed; the paper fluttered down and the hand remained fixed like a claw. Then Maurice Selby gave a lurch forward, uttered a cry like the howl of an animal, and

228

fell headlong down the stairs.

Oliver reached him too late to break his fall. He went down on one knee and carefully turned the inert figure. Behind him he could hear Mrs Selby's gasping breath. He glanced up at her, and she tried to speak.

'Is he . . .' She stared in horror at the trickle of blood beginning to spread on the marble floor. 'He's not . . . not dead?'

'No. I think he's badly hurt. I don't think we should risk moving him. Is the telephone connected?'

'Yes.'

'Then ring for an ambulance.'

They waited in silence. They did not have to wait long. They heard the siren and then the sound of the engine and then the voices of the men at the door. Mrs Selby looked at Oliver.

'You'll come to the hospital with me?' she begged.

'Of course.'

As the stretcher bearers, with their unconscious burden, reached the terrace, Oliver saw Jeanne and Austin running up the path. They waited at the top as the men went by. Austin looked from the figure on the stretcher to Mrs Selby and then to Oliver, silently asking for an explanation. It came from Mrs Selby.

'He fell downstairs,' she said. Her voice was steady. 'If you want to know what made him fall, you'll have to ask that woman whose name

I can't remember. The one who also fell downstairs.'

'Mrs Clermont?' Austin asked in a dazed voice.

'Yes. Whoever pushed her, pushed him,' Mrs Selby said stonily, and followed the stretcher bearers to the waiting ambulance.

CHAPTER NINE

Maurice Selby was unconscious for three hours. Throughout this time, his wife sat silent and almost immobile in the waiting room of the Hine hospital, and Oliver stayed with her.

At about half past eight, a tray with sandwiches and coffee was brought to them. Mrs Selby ignored it. Oliver poured out coffee and offered it to her, but she shook her head. He drank some, but he could not bring himself to eat; each time he felt a pang of hunger, he remembered the look on Maurice Selby's face just before he fell down the stairs, and all desire for food left him.

At about ten o'clock, Mrs Selby was summoned to her husband's bedside. She was not away long. When she returned, she spoke briefly to Oliver.

'We can go now. Thanks for staying.'

'How is he?'

'Two ribs broken, dislocated shoulder,

which they're not worried about. Shock, which they are.'

'Did you talk to him?'

'Yes. He didn't speak. Except once, to the doctors, to ask how long he'd be kept here. They said they didn't know.'

'Didn't he say anything at all to you?'

'No. He just lay there staring at the ceiling. I told him I'd come back and see him in the morning.'

He drove her to the hotel. The entrance hall looked emptier than ever. In the alcove where Mr Royce had sat every night, he now sat with Elva, and Oliver with difficulty remembered that she had come to dine with him. Mrs Selby did not pause; she went to the lift and left Oliver to join the others.

'The news,' Elva told him, 'is all over the hotel. How is Mr Selby?'

'Broken ribs and a dislocated shoulder. And shock. I'd like to get back to the cottage. If you'd like a lift—'

Elva rose with undisguised relief.

'Yes, please.'

'Before you go,' Mr Royce said to Oliver, 'I'd like to hear about this accident. What exactly happened?'

'God knows. I don't suppose anyone will ever know for certain. He was coming down the stairs when he stopped, looked over his shoulder with what I can only describe as terror, and then came down with a crash. As they say old Mrs Clermont did.'

'That's what comes of listening to rumours,' Elva said, and turned to say good night to her father. 'Thank you for the dinner.'

'I'm afraid it wasn't a very interesting evening for you,' he said.

'It was more than interesting,' Elva told him, and something in her tone brought a flush to his face. He walked to the door with her and waited until she and Oliver were in the car before turning back into the hall.

'You're looking terrible,' she told Oliver. 'Did you stay all the time at the hospital with Mrs Selby?'

'Yes. I could hardly leave her there alone.'

'I suppose not.'

When they reached the cottage, Austin glanced at Oliver's face and suggested brandy.

'You look washed out,' he said.

'Did you eat anything?' Jeanne asked.

'No.'

'I could make you some cold meat sandwiches. Would you eat them?'

'Yes. Thanks.'

'What was the damage?' Austin asked.

Oliver told him. Asked for details of how the accident had occurred, he gave as full an account as he could.

'Panic?' Austin asked as he ended. 'And if so, ghost, or rumours of ghosts?'

'I've given up,' Oliver said. 'I'm thankful that his wife and I were standing at the bottom

232

of the stairs when he fell down them. If we'd been behind him, or if she and I hadn't seen the thing happening, we'd have found it difficult to make people believe the story.'

'How's he going to face his workmen after this?' Roberta asked. 'And if there's a ghost, which we'll soon have to admit there must be, why is it so choosey about who it pushes down the stairs? Why not one of us?'

'Anybody's guess,' Austin said. 'How did your evening go?' he asked Elva. 'Did you find out anything you wanted to know?'

'Yes.'

'He talked?' Roberta asked.

'No.'

'Then you guessed?'

'No. I reasoned. I know why he came and what he's doing here. All he told me was when he was leaving. He's going away on the evening train tomorrow. And my reasoning leads me to suspect that he isn't travelling alone.'

She picked up the handbag that Roberta had lent her for the evening, and said that she was going to bed.

'You can't leave us in the air,' Austin protested.

'I'm not leaving you in the air for long. I want to work out my conclusions by myself. In the morning, I'll tell you what I think, and time will prove whether I'm right or not. Good night.'

She left the others speculating, but they did

not dwell long on the subject of Mr Royce; Maurice Selby, and what had happened to him, was of more interest to them. But it was felt that until he gave his own account of what had happened, it was useless to try and reach any conclusions.

Oliver slept badly, and when at last he fell asleep, dreamt of the look he had seen on Maurice Selby's face. He woke early, and decided to have a swim before breakfast. But as he was going downstairs, he heard sounds in the kitchen and found Jeanne and the twins seated at the table.

'Good morning. You're early,' he said.

'It was such a heavenly morning. We decided we'd have a drink and then go down and swim.'

'I'll join you. Any coffee to spare?'

They went down the path together, the twins and Duke leading the way. The twins plunged straight into the sea, Duke between them; they had discovered that he was better than a rubber duck, as they could hold on to his collar and be towed out and back again.

Oliver, instead of swimming, sat on the sand and gazed absently out to sea.

'Aren't you coming in?' Jeanne asked him.

'Not yet. Sit down. I want to ask you something.'

She sat down and he turned to face her, a puzzled look on his face.

'This might sound silly,' he said, 'but it's an

234

idea I got last night, and I can't get rid of it. It's about Elva's father.'

'Go on,' she invited.

Her tone made him look at her with more attention.

'Do you know what I'm going to say?' he asked.

'No. But I had an idea too—such an unlikely one that I was going to keep it to myself.'

'Was it about him only, or about him and someone else?'

'It was about him—and Mrs Selby.'

'I'm glad you said it first,' he told her. 'I thought—in Boris's words—that I was letting my imagination run away with me. I've got a feeling they're linked in some way. But how? I've seen him myself sitting alone in his alcove, his eyes glued to his book. They've passed each other without a word. When she went up to her room on the night of Austin's party, they came face to face at the lift—and not a sign from either of them. If they know one another, why the secrecy?'

'Her jealous husband?'

'That did, of course, occur to me. But he could hardly object to her talking to a man staying in the same hotel. Elva must have come to some kind of solution, but I'd like to work it out for myself. She isn't the only one with reasoning powers. How far had you got?'

'Only that Elva's father was here because Mrs Selby was here. But it can't be so if they

235

say nothing to each other all day.'

'How about nights? Work it out. They meet, he's attracted ... No, that means he didn't know her before he came here, and I'm more and more certain that he did.'

'Do the rooms, any of the rooms, communicate?'

'No. Not the bedrooms. But the bathrooms do. I mean that you can get from the bathrooms out on to a narrow balcony that runs along the back of the building. It's a fire escape. So they could have got to one another's rooms. I've always felt that she had something on her mind that wasn't her husband. So it might be Elva's father—and that's as far as I can go. Elva'll have to supply the whole answer. If she can. Now come and swim.'

When they went up to breakfast, neither Elva nor Roberta was down.

'After breakfast,' Oliver said, 'I think I'll go along to the hospital. I might be allowed to see Selby.'

'Why do you want to see him?' Jeanne asked. 'Why don't you just telephone to ask how he is?'

'I want to see if he'll talk about the accident. I can't forget that look on his face. I don't see how he can dismiss it as a simple fall. I saw him, and his wife saw him. He looked half-crazed with fear.'

'Will he remember? Doesn't concussion

sometimes—'

'He'll remember. Mrs Clermont remembered. But she was willing, not to say eager to talk. I don't know whether he'll be. Anyhow, I'll go to the hospital.'

'Will you take Mrs Selby with you?'

'No. She can take herself by taxi. Or she can ask Austin for a lift. I'd rather go alone.'

There were a few people in the waiting room of the hospital, but Mrs Selby was not one of them. To his enquiries he was informed that Mr Selby was seeing nobody. Mrs Selby had been with him for a few minutes, but had left the hospital about ten minutes ago.

Oliver walked out to his car. Ten minutes. He must have passed her on the road—she had presumably been in a taxi.

He drove to the hotel and asked the reception clerk to put a call through to Mrs Selby's room.

'Mrs Selby is not in, sir.'

'I know she went to the hospital. I wondered if she was back.'

'She returned, sir, but she went out again with Mr Parkes.'

Oliver drove away. There was no point, he thought, in going round the town looking for them. He would go home and try to get in touch with her at lunch time.

When he turned on to the promontory road, he saw Austin's car turning into the gateway of the cottage. He parked his car behind it, reflecting that Austin had not had time to drive her very far—perhaps only to do an errand in the town. Then he opened the kitchen door, and through the archway saw Mrs Selby seated beside one of the little tables.

She was not alone. Elva was beside her. Roberta had just finished her breakfast. Jeanne poured out some of the coffee that was left, and Austin carried it to Mrs Selby.

'Hot and strong,' he said. 'Get that inside you.'

She looked as though she needed it. She raised her eyes and saw Oliver, but said nothing; she drank the coffee in slow sips, absorbed in her own thoughts. Not until she had finished, and given the cup back to Austin, did she speak.

'Thank you. I needed that.' She looked at Oliver. 'You went to the hospital?'

'Yes. No visitors. They told me you'd been there. How is he?'

'About the same. They're transferring him to the Beulah Hospital in London. He's going this afternoon by ambulance.'

'Are you going with him?'

'No.'

'If you'd rather not travel in the ambulance, I could drive you up.'

'Thank you—but no.'

'Did he talk about the accident?'

'No. I'm not sure that he ever will.' She opened her handbag, groped and then looked

238

round the room. 'Can anyone give me a cigarette?'

Roberta supplied one and Austin supplied a light.

'Thank you.' She inhaled deeply and gratefully. 'That's better.'

'At mid-morning,' Austin told her, 'my aunts used to ring for a glass of Madeira. If it isn't too soon after the coffee—'

'No Madeira. I'm going to do some talking. When I'm through, I might ask for a brandy. But not yet.' She looked at Oliver. 'Parson's House,' she said, 'is up for sale.'

Nobody could find anything to say; only their expressions indicated the impact that the brief announcement had produced. Then Austin's voice was heard.

'You're . . . you're selling it?'

'It isn't mine to sell. My husband is putting it on the market.'

'At once?'

'Yes. I don't know why. He didn't tell me. He said it was a mistake not to have sold it when his brother died.'

'But the whole idea was to get back into the house,' Oliver said. 'Didn't he give any reason for selling?'

'No. You know, and I know why he's selling—but he'll never admit that that's his reason. When I asked him what made him fall down those stairs, he said he lost his footing. I couldn't leave it at that. I asked him why he had looked over his shoulder. He said he hadn't done anything of the kind. But when he said it, his face looked the way it had looked before he fell. He's lying there with only one idea in his mind: to get away. Away from Rocksea, away from the house. He's selling the house and the furniture and he isn't coming back.'

'That was what you wanted,' Oliver said.

'Yes. That was what I wanted. But I feel like someone who lit a match and started a prairie fire. I didn't know it would turn out like this. How could I know?'

'When you say "I", you mean "we", don't you?' Elva asked her.

'Yes. There had to be someone else. How could I have known what would happen? That fool of a woman, Pandora, opened the box and let out all the evils of the world. We lit our match and out came the spirits. Do we here in this room believe in ghosts? If we haven't been convinced yet, we should be. I wanted that house to be haunted, and haunted it is. God knows what I wouldn't give to be back in London, back at the time before it all began. But it's too late. The spirits have been let out.'

'Was it your idea?' Elva asked.

'Yes. I wasn't in a state to think rationally. The gallery I worked in had closed. The owners had always kept a suite of rooms there, and when they were away, which was most of the time, I used the rooms to . . . to entertain

240

my friends. The gallery was my escape from all the things I didn't like in life. My husband, chiefly. Those rooms were warm, safe and comfortable—the ideal place for making love. And then suddenly there was no gallery.'

'But still a place for making love,' Elva reminded her. 'Five bedrooms, five bathrooms and several other rooms which were warm and safe and comfortable.'

'No, not safe. To be seen going in or coming out, to be unavailable when my husband wanted me, to be seen by the servants, recognised—no, not safe. There was only one way in which I could go there, but I couldn't get him to agree.'

'I can understand that,' Elva said. 'How long have you been trying?'

'Ever since your mother died. He said I could have everything in the world—except marriage. I couldn't move him, and so I married Maurice Selby. I couldn't face life without money. Independence is for women who can look after themselves, women with some kind of training, women with guts. I couldn't make a decent living, and I'm not built to carry on a series of affairs. I had fallen in love, and I wanted the security of marriage. So I married Selby, and he thought I lived with him, but I only lived in the rooms at the gallery. And then he sold the house. So the man I loved was to be in London and I was to be here, and I knew what the house here

241

meant to Maurice and I knew there was no hope of getting him to give it up. All I could think of was finding some good reason I could use for refusing to live in it. And I thought of ghosts. If the house were haunted . . . There didn't have to be ghosts—I thought. Rumours would do. But who would spread them?'

'Mr Cristall,' said Elva.

'Yes. Your father knew him. The restaurant was close to his house and he often dined there and he knew that anything Mr Cristall heard would be passed on. But London was too far away; the rumours would have to start here. So your father came down and took a room at the hotel and talked to Mr Cristall, and it was easy to bring the conversation round to Parson's House and say that it had a reputation in London for the odd things that happened to people who worked at the house. It doesn't sound like a plan that could work—but you all know how well it worked.'

She paused and with shaking fingers took another cigarette from Roberta.

'But you know the truth about the ghosts,' Austin said. 'So why mention spirits?'

She stared at him for some moments before answering. When she spoke, her eyes were on Oliver.

'You were there,' she said slowly. 'You saw him as he fell. I shall believe all my life that there was something there, something you and I—thank God—couldn't see. It'—she paused,

242

shivering—'it might have been different with all the others. They'd been conditioned. They'd been fed on rumours. But not Maurice. He wouldn't even listen when Mr Quinter came to London and tried to tell him what people were saying. All he heard was that the job wasn't getting done. When he went into Parson's House yesterday, all he was thinking of was furniture. When he went back for that paper and we saw him at the top of the stairs, he looked just the way he always looked. And then something turned him into a ... a cringing, panic-stricken animal. You yourself, all of you in this room, can make what you like of it. I can't forget it and I never will and I don't understand how Oliver will be able to either. And Maurice ...'

Oliver broke a long silence.

'Have they told you how long he'll be in hospital?' he asked.

'Not long, they said. There's not much wrong physically. But you won't see him down here again. And you won't see me.'

'When are you going to London?' Austin asked.

'On this evening's train.'

'And not alone,' Elva said.

'No. Not alone.' Mrs Selby turned to face her. 'Do you want to know it all?'

'Yes. If you don't mind.'

'We met at the gallery two years ago. A friend of his brought him in. While the friend
243

looked at pictures, your father and I talked. He told me his house wasn't far from the gallery. He told me he had a wife. He didn't mention a daughter.'

'It frequently slipped his mind.'

'I was free. I fell in love. I didn't know how he felt about me until your mother died. He went to the Caribbean for a time and then he came back—and came to see me. After that, we went on meeting. I was happy, because I was certain—at first—that he'd marry me. When I began to believe that he wouldn't, I got into a panic—and married Maurice Selby. After that, I had to make sure that Maurice never suspected anything. And then the gallery was sold and Maurice's house was sold and I had the choice of living down here and never seeing your father—or leaving Maurice and being happy with a man who might leave me. I couldn't face either prospect. The rumours of ghosts was a last desperate attempt to keep things the way they were. The idea was mine, but it was your father who thought of Mr Cristall. He wouldn't have come here if he hadn't seen a notice in the papers about your going to South America. He thought you were out of the way, and so it was safe to come. Nobody here had ever seen him. Until I heard your name on the night of the birthday party, we had no suspicion . . .'

'What happens now?' Elva asked.

'I can't do without him. I'll tell Maurice

when he's on his feet again. And then I'll move into your father's house and wait for my divorce, and after that I'll try and break down his resistance to marriage.'

'I don't think you'll do that,' Elva said. 'He won't marry you.'

'He married your mother.'

'That,' Elva said, 'is what is generally believed. I believed it myself until I was eighteen. But in fact he didn't. He was a very faithful non-husband; my mother told me that he didn't need, didn't want, couldn't cope with more than one woman at a time. She had to watch him, but she never lost him. She never tried to change him. As you must know by now, he's generous, to himself and to his non-wife; he's even-tempered, rather dull and perhaps insensitive, but his chief characteristic is his inability to understand that he has any responsibilities beyond his own welfare. If you're going to take him on permanently, you may as well know what you're getting. It isn't that he evades his paternal or civic duties—he simply doesn't know they exist. If my mother didn't change him, I don't think anybody else will. You'll have to take him as he is.'

Mrs Selby spoke unhesitatingly.

'That's all right,' she said. 'I'll take him as he is.'

CHAPTER TEN

Maurice Selby's accident had the effect of sweeping away all rumours in Rocksea. There was general acceptance of the fact that Parson's House was haunted. Proof was proof; if a man put his own house up for sale because he was afraid to live in it, there was something inside it that couldn't be explained away. There were still many who maintained that they didn't believe in ghosts, but among these, there was none who was not prepared to concede that there was something peculiar about the place.

Austin wasted no time in going to the firm of house agents in Exeter who were dealing with the sale. Early on the morning after the departure of Mrs Selby and Mr Royce, he was at the cottage.

'I'd like you to come with me,' he told Oliver. 'It's Saturday—they'll only be open until midday. I could leave it till Monday—I don't suppose there'll be a queue lining up to make an offer for a haunted house—but I'd like to make sure of being the first.'

Oliver, finishing dressing in his room, selected a tie and put it on.

'You're really going to buy it?' he asked.

'Did you imagine I'd let anybody else get hold of it?'

'I wasn't sure.'

'Then you should have been. I was certain you'd be after it yourself.'

'What would I use for money?'

'I thought you'd have the sense to ask me to buy it and let you pay me back over a period of years. Your grandfather built it, your mother was born in it and we all had some good times in it.'

'It's too big for a bachelor.'

'So I thought. It's just the right size for a bachelor with twins.'

'You're anticipating.'

'I don't think I am. I've been using my eyes, and what I think is that if you let her go, you'll be a fool, and if you don't settle down with her in Parson's House, you'll be a bigger one. Why don't you put it to her?'

'I will.'

'But not this morning. We've got to get to Exeter. I want to know what price they've put on a house that's got ghosts in it.'

'Would you live in it?'

'Of course I would. If you don't want it, that's just what I'll do: live in it. You don't think I believe in Mrs Selby's spirits, do you?'

'I was wondering.'

'Then stop wondering, and don't let Selby's accident leave you with any silly ideas. What hit him was the realisation of the way he'd mucked up his relations with David. Think: He hadn't entered the house since his row with his brother and your mother. When he did, when

247

he saw for the first time that he could have been a frequent visitor, could have come down on visits, even kept a room in the house as you do here, he realised what he'd been missing, and realised that it was only his jealousy of your mother that had made him act the way he did. I don't wonder he fell downstairs. But if you want to believe a ghost pushed him, then go ahead and believe it. We've all got a crazy streak, some streakier than others.'

Oliver brushed his hair, put down the brush, and turned.

'If you're interested,' he said, 'my view on ghosts is that people create their own.'

'You mean there wasn't a ghost there to push Maurice Selby down the stairs—he merely thought there was.'

'Yes.'

'Then we're in agreement. But we'll keep our views to ourselves while we're at the house agents. We're going to be confirmed ghost-believers, making an offer for a haunted house. We're going to take the line that nobody's likely to want it but ourselves. Come on; let's go.'

Roberta, walking up from the beach shortly afterwards, paused to look up at Parson's House. The men were still working; she wondered what they thought of this latest development. About the future of the house, she had no doubts; Austin would buy it. What he would do with it, she could not guess, but if he was seeing her in it with him, she would tell

248

him that he was seeing double.

Elva, still on the beach with Jeanne and the twins, was also speculating.

'Does a house sell more cheaply if it's believed to be haunted, or does that put the price up?' she asked Jeanne.

'I don't know. More cheaply, I think.'

'Unless a few sensation-seekers go after it. But Austin will buy it.'

'Are you sure?'

'Quite sure. He certainly wouldn't let it go to anybody else.'

'If he did, it would be nice in one way.'

'In which way?' Elva was putting the finishing touches to a sand castle that the twins had abandoned. 'To live in it himself?'

'I was thinking how nice it would be if . . . I mean, it's so obvious that he's in love with Roberta. Isn't it?'

'Quite obvious.'

'Then if he bought the house, wouldn't it be wonderful if they got married and lived there?'

'It certainly would.' Elva patted a tower into position. 'But they won't.'

'But if they're in love?'

'He is.'

'Isn't she?'

'In love? Yes, she's in love.'

'Then—?'

'But not with Austin. You're not very observant, are you? She's been in love with Oliver for years.'

Through the heavy silence that fell, Jeanne recognised faint, faraway, familiar echoes—the laughter of the twins, the inward rush and the breaking of the waves, the cry of the gulls. She saw Elva get to her feet and pick up her towel and turn to go up to the house.

Roberta . . . and Oliver.

Oliver . . . and Roberta. Roberta, who had brought her here, welcomed her, provided a temporary home. Roberta . . .

And Oliver.

Numbed, she did her best to cast her mind back to the past weeks. Unobservant? What had there been to observe?

Oliver—yes, she had observed Oliver. What she thought she had observed was his growing feeling for her. But the reality lay in those years during which she had been away, years during which the others had been together, here or in London. She had been an outsider, knowing little of their way of life—and nothing of their feelings.

She was thankful for the solitude, thankful for a little time in which to face this devastating blow. It had been foolish, childish, madness to imagine that her future, and the children's, could have found so swift and so simple a solution.

She had no doubt as to what she would do. She would go away. She would go to France, as she had intended to do, as she wished with all her heart she had done when she left Canada.

To have gone without meeting Oliver again . . .

She stayed on the beach as long as she could. When at last she went up with the twins to the cottage, she opened the door of the kitchen to see a group who seemed to her, for the first confused moments, to be sharing her unhappiness. Elva and Roberta were seated at the table, sunk in gloom. Oliver, his expression grim, was watching Austin, who was pacing up and down, misery on his face.

'What's happened?' she asked apprehensively.

Austin came to halt in front of her.

'It's gone,' he said.

'What's gone?'

'The house. Parson's House. Sold.'

'Somebody . . . somebody else bought it?'

'Yes.'

'Who?'

'Dent and Son, Builders. They were at the agents as soon as the doors were opened. There's no hitch. They've got it. It's gone.'

The extent of the disaster—for as such they all regarded it—sank slowly into Jeanne's mind. Parson's House, which they had thought of as their own, was lost to them. The rooms in which they still pictured Lorna and David, the rooms in which they themselves had lived and been so happy, were to be occupied by Reg and Dot, Mum and Dad.

'Funny to think,' Roberta said, 'that if the Selbys came back, we'd welcome them.'

'There must be *something* we can do,' Austin said desperately.

'You sound like Boris,' Elva said. 'What'll she say when she hears about her new neighbours?'

'She's heard. We met her and told her,' Oliver said. 'She's going to take it hard. She's nearer to Parson's House than we are, and they've got a clear view of her patio and her windows on that side.'

'She won't feel like conducting her madrigal singers tomorrow,' Roberta commented. 'How did she manage to rope in thirty-eight people to stand round chirping "Come Cuckoo Come"?'

Oliver looked at her.

'Thirty-eight?' he asked.

'So she said.'

'Thirty-eight people going there tomorrow to sing madrigals?'

'That's right. Their first rehearsal. Can you imagine the row?'

Oliver turned slowly and gazed at Austin. The eyes of the two men met, but no words passed. Then Austin answered the unspoken suggestion.

'We'd have to move fast.'

'We'll start now.' Oliver, no longer inactive, his expression firm and purposeful, seized Roberta's arm and began to pull her to her feet. 'Come with me,' he ordered. 'I've got a job for you.' When she resisted, he spoke in a burst of irritation. 'I said *Come*. Come on, come on, come *on*.'

'Where to?'

'To wherever you keep your paint pots. Will you *hurry*?'

'But—'

'Why do you always *argue*? We sit around here like a collection of castaways, and when we get an idea, you bring out a lot of reasons why the damn thing won't work. I know it won't work, but we can at least try it, can't we?'

'Try what?'

'There you go again. Will you shut up and *move*, for God's sake?'

He hurried her up the stairs. The door of her room banged behind them.

'Interesting, but uninformative,' Elva remarked. 'He's got some kind of—'

She was interrupted by a shout from the landing.

'Austin!' Oliver came thundering down the stairs. 'Don't just stand there! Go and talk to Quinter. Tell him what's happened and tell him we want his help. In the form of his notice board.'

'His—?'

'What's the matter with everybody this morning? Wake up, wake up. His *notice* board. His sign. The thing he put up outside the house when he was working on it. I suppose you saw it?'

'Yes.'

'Well, I don't want the sign, but I want the support.'

'Support?'

'That's what I said: support. Tell him to detach it from the sign and then bring it round here. And tell him I want another signboard made.'

'Another signboard?'

'Can't you follow the simplest directions? I want, first, the support for the board. I want, second, a board. I don't for the moment, want the two joined together. I'll do the joining later. Now will you get moving?'

Austin went out. Oliver, halfway up the stairs, turned and came down again.

'You,' he said to Elva, 'go over and tell Boris we're going to join the Madrigal singers tomorrow. On one condition. The condition being that she holds the rehearsal in the patio. Tell her this is vitally important, so important that she must see to it that it doesn't rain.' He turned to Jeanne. 'Your job is to keep the food and drink flowing,' he said.

The rest of the day was confused. Roberta remained in her room. Austin took up dinner on a tray for himself and for her. Elva returned from Vistamar with a request to Jeanne for help in the form of cakes for the singers' tea on the following day. Jeanne threw herself thankfully into the task, giving the twins dough to form into animal shapes that could be put into the oven.

254

Of Oliver there was no sign. Elva thought that he had gone to see Mr Quinter, but he telephoned during the evening to say that he was meeting somebody for dinner in Exeter.

'A lawyer,' Austin guessed. 'It won't do any good. There's no legal way out of this.'

On Sunday morning, Jeanne walked to Vistamar with the cakes she had made. Lady Cressing took the basket with gratitude.

'Trotter and I hadn't the heart to do much baking,' she said. 'Oh Jeanne, my dear, what are we going to do? Can you imagine those terrible, terrible people living at Parson's House? We've seen enough of them, heard enough of them to know what kind of neighbours they're going to be. They say the most wounding things about us, in loud voices so that we can hear. I don't mind for myself, but it hurts poor old Trotter. If only, if only it could have been a nice builder like Mr Quinter, such a good friend, such a *gentleman*. And with such a nice wife, who would have been so nice to have next door. But those Dents . . . a *disaster*!'

'Yes,' Jeanne agreed.

'You're looking pale,' Lady Cressing told her. 'We've all had a shock. Thank Heaven for the madrigals this afternoon; it'll do us good to sing some of the sadness out of us.'

She walked to the gate with Jeanne. Austin, driving by, stopped to speak to them.

'I've told Jeanne what I think of the whole

255

dreadful business,' Lady Cressing said. 'When I think of those people about to install themselves in—'

'Not about to,' Austin corrected. 'Installed.'

She stared at him, her eyes widening.

'You can't mean—'

'No heavy luggage yet, but suitcases with bits and pieces. They've settled down for the day and it won't be long before they settle down for good.'

'But surely—'

'They own the house. There are of course some minor matters like payment and lawyers' fees and agents' fees to be settled, but that doesn't seem to them sufficient reason for not enjoying a nice Sunday in the house. What's the difference? They've been using it every day, in and out, upstairs and down, all the time the work's been going on.'

'Apart from the sheer tastelessness of—' She broke off and compressed her lips. 'Something will have to be done.'

'Agreed,' Austin said. 'And now a small item: can you check the time of the rehearsal?'

'Three-thirty sharp. I hope you'll all be punctual.'

'On the dot. It's to be in the patio?'

'Yes. That was a very good idea. If only I had a larger terrace—'

'No. Too windy,' Austin objected. 'The sound would be carried away.' He opened the car door. 'Get in, Jeanne. Not far to walk, but

256

quicker to drive.'

Outside the door of the kitchen Jeanne saw, propped against the wall, a large blank notice board. Close by were the wooden supports. They went in to find Oliver coming down the stairs holding one side of a very large canvas. The other side was held by Roberta.

'Wait. I'll give you a hand,' Austin said.

'Be careful. I'm not sure that it's dry,' Roberta warned him.

They propped the canvas against the board. Jeanne saw some outsize notes of music on lines that stretched across the entire width. At one side stood two figures, rather like carol singers, holding sheets of music. Placed in the centre, in lettering which Austin said could be seen from here to Land's End, was:

THE ROCKSEA MADRIGAL CLUB.
NON-MEMBERS WELCOME.
DAILY REHEARSALS.
FOR DETAILS OF MEMBERSHIP
APPLY WITHIN

They stood admiring it.

'As soon as we've had something to eat,' Oliver said, 'we'll take it across to Boris and ask her what she thinks of it. But we'll rig it up first. Then it'll be too late for her to suggest alterations.'

Nobody but the twins showed very much interest in lunch. Only Oliver and Austin knew

257

why the board was to be placed at the gate of Vistamar, and they showed no disposition to answer questions about details. As soon as they had eaten, they went outside, and the sound of hammering was heard.

When the board was in place at Lady Cressing's gate, she was led out to inspect it.

'Be careful what you say,' Roberta warned her. 'I painted it.'

'It's beautiful,' Lady Cressing declared. 'Such a good idea, and such a wonderful advertisement for the club. Tomorrow, I shall have a glass put over it, and then I shall have it taken to the Club's permanent premises. I long to see the faces of the members as they arrive and see this imposing sign.'

The members, arriving, were genuinely impressed. Austin and Oliver watched them as they came, singly or in groups, through the gate, stopping to admire the sign and then walking on to be greeted by their hostess. They were then passed on to Elva, to be led to the patio.

'Now listen to me,' Oliver told Austin, when the last of the thirty-eight had arrived. 'The Dent lot went out. When you see that yellow pantechnicon of theirs coming back, let me know.'

'How d'you know they're coming back?'

'They went out to lunch. I heard. You can't help hearing, but today, I wanted to hear. They talked of a picnic lunch on the beach, but Dot refused. She doesn't want to be brown; she wants to stay pink-and-white, which explains why they've left the beach to us up to now. They decided to lunch in town. So they'll be back. Keep looking.'

At twenty-five minutes past three, Austin made his report.

'Yellow car in sight.'

'Good. Now here's what you do,' Oliver said. 'Listen carefully.'

A few moments later, Austin was bounding towards the gate. He ran in the direction of Parson's House, slowing down and entering its gate just as the Dents were getting out of the yellow car. He went up to them and spoke with eager friendliness.

'Oh, *good*! We all hoped you'd be back in time. You saw the notice?'

The older Dent regarded him with a surly expression.

'What notice? D'you mean that great board outside the house next door—is that what you're talking about?'

'That's it. Madrigal club. You will join, won't you?' Austin said, and made it sound a settled thing. 'You ought to be getting along, you know—we're almost ready to begin.'

Without answering, Mr Dent strode to the gate and stood staring at the notice. With him went his wife and the two younger Dents.

'D'you think I'm going to let that thing stay up there?' he demanded. 'A bloody great thing

259

stuck up where we can see it from our windows?'

'It was specially done for Lady Cressing,' Austin told them. 'She's so looking forward to having you as members.'

'Then she's going to be disappointed,' Dot said vindictively. 'I'm not wearing madrigals this season. Who's going to sing them—you and her?'

'Oh, by no means! There are—let me see—thirty-eight plus five, that makes forty-three at the moment, but the club is still very young. We hope to double our numbers.'

'Forty-three? Forty-three?' Mrs Dent senior said in a tone of horror. 'You don't mean there's forty-three in there, all going to sing?'

'Not *in* there; *out* there,' Austin corrected. 'Lady Cressing thinks it's far healthier to hold rehearsals in the open when the weather allows it. Are you sure you won't come and join in?'

'I won't come and join out, either,' the younger Dent said with force. 'You can go and tell the old . . . you can tell her so.' He turned away. 'Come on, Dot. Come on, Mum and Dad.'

Austin returned with springy step to the patio. Lady Cressing had mounted a strong-looking wooden box that had been placed in front of one of the drawing room windows, and was tapping the window sill with her baton. Roberta and Jeanne, who had been giving out sheets of music, took their places in one of the lines of singers. On chairs at one side of the patio sat the twins, wide-eyed and expectant.

'Let me for the first time welcome the members of this Club to our first full rehearsal,' Lady Cressing said, her voice ringing out over the assembled singers. 'This is a really splendid beginning. I hope you all admired the beautiful notice that Miss Murray—here she is, the very charming young lady in green—painted for us. I'm sure you would all like to express your appreciation.'

They expressed it. The sound of clapping seemed magnified in the patio, and Oliver glanced at Austin. This, he seemed to say, was going to prove an even noisier session than they had hoped.

'You will see,' trumpeted Lady Cressing, 'that we are going to begin with a madrigal which has words translated from the French. I chose it because it recalls the sea beside which we all live, though I'm thankful to say that we don't very often experience storms of the intensity you'll be singing about. It isn't a difficult madrigal, but it isn't, on the other hand, one for beginners. When I met each of you at the enrolment ceremony, I realised that many of you were experienced in this form of singing. I thought we might begin, experimentally, with this piece, and later we can place beginners beside the old hands. We'll take it from the beginning: "Storm cloud, rising o'er the sea", to the end of page two: "crash of angry waves". Are we all ready? Trotter, may I have the note?'

In the drawing room, Trotter, stationed at the piano, jabbed several times at the note. Lady Cressing picked it up and passed it on to the singers.

'Mmm, Mmm—altos, got it? Mm. A little sharp, I think. That's better. Just try it all together.'

'Mmm, Mmm,' droned the choir.

'Splendid. Four beats in a bar, you come in on three. Are you ready? One, two, THREE, four; one, two, THREE . . .'

Her baton rose and fell. A volume of sound rose from the singers, so loud that Austin claimed later that if he had been wearing a hat, it would have been blown off.

The sound was not altogether harmonious. Lady Cressing stopped them with some clicks of the baton.

'Good, but not good enough,' she told them. 'The sopranos must remember to wait for those two empty bars. Let's try it again.'

They tried it several times. Lady Cressing was patient, but she was also a perfectionist; she wanted, she said, their very best.

It was about twenty to four when Austin directed Oliver's attention to the wall between Vistamar and Parson's House. Hands were clutching the top as someone attempted to get high enough to look over it. There was a glimpse of Reg Dent's long fair hair—and then the hands slipped away.

'He'll be round,' Oliver murmured during a bar's rest.

It was not Reg Dent, but his father who appeared, purple with rage, at the entrance to the patio. His mouth was seen opening and shutting, but not until Lady Cressing had caught sight of him and clicked the choir to silence could his words be heard.

'I won't have it!' he yelled. 'You can't make this sort of disturbance in a quiet neighbourhood. I won't stand for it! D'you hear me?'

The only thing that could make Lady Cressing happier than when she was conducting her madrigal singers was the opportunity of crossing swords with her hated neighbour. She addressed him from her eminence.

'Are you addressing me?'

'Who else? You're responsible for this hollering, aren't you? We've stood enough.'

Her eyes went from his to the faces of his family, visible at the windows overlooking the patio. The choir waited hopefully; the Dents had not made themselves loved in the town.

'Kindly go away,' Lady Cressing said. 'You're disturbing us.'

'Disturbing? That's a laugh! *You* talk to *me* about disturbing?'

'You are an intruder, and my dogs are good

guards,' she warned him.

As well as being good guards, they were interested spectators. They had been sitting round the wooden box, lulled by the singing. Now they were on their feet, their eyes on Mr Dent, their ears at attention.

'To hell with you and your dogs,' yelled Mr Dent, now beside himself. 'If you don't stop this caterwauling, I'll get the police.'

Curzon took two steps forward.

'No, Curzon,' said Lady Cressing.

There were forty-three witnesses to swear, later, that what she had said was No, Curzon and not Go, Curzon. But the dog had made his own estimate of the situation, and with a snarl, had sprung in the direction of the intruder. Mr Dent turned and ran. Curzon accompanied him to the gate and helped him through it with a nip at the seat of his trousers. His hand clutching the spot, Mr Dent vanished down the road.

'Now let us resume,' Lady Cressing said.

They resumed. They were able to sing two whole pages before the next interruption came. This time, it came from the other side of the wall, and it came from Reg Dent. He was at a low window, leaning out, shaking his fist and shouting. At the window next to the one at which he stood, the other three members of the family could be seen watching.

'Shut up,' he screamed. 'Shut up, the whole bunch of you!' He shook his hair out of his eyes. 'Any more of it, and I'll—'

He stopped abruptly. For a few seconds there was a puzzled look on his face. His mouth hung open. Then he gave a sudden lurch forward. A deathly silence reigned in the patio.

There were forty-three witnesses to state exactly what happened next. But the well-known inaccuracy of eye-witnesses was proved by the fact that while several people stated that his hand was on the window-catch, and the window opened suddenly to its fullest extent, carrying him with it, there were others who were prepared to swear that something, someone had pushed him from behind. Why else did he look over his shoulder for that fearful second, before he fell?

Nobody would ever come to any definite conclusion. Not even his parents and his wife would ever be able to decide exactly what had occurred. But Reg Dent, lying moaning on the flagstones, had no doubt as to how he got there. As he was borne away by the same ambulance that had removed Maurice Selby, as he was driven to the same hospital and placed in the same bed as that which Maurice Selby had occupied, he stated clearly that he had been pushed out. Since his wife and his parents were some feet away at the next window, and as there was nobody else inside the house, Rocksea was left to draw its own conclusions.

CHAPTER ELEVEN

The Sunday of the madrigal rehearsal was succeeded by a brief interval during which the people of Rocksea speculated on the future of Parson's House. Among the Dents, older and younger, there was no need for speculation. They had reached a unanimous decision on the way to Hine Hospital.

The withdrawal of the workmen on the following day was correctly interpreted by Austin Parkes, and this time, he made certain that nothing interfered with the negotiations leading to the change of ownership. Before the week ended, he had become the proprietor of Parson's House.

'All due to me,' Oliver said with a certain smugness.

'Rot.' Austin snorted. 'You couldn't have foreseen it would work.'

'Of course I couldn't—any more than Mrs Selby could have foreseen that a crazy scheme like hers would work. The ideas in both cases sprang from desperation. There was no time to think, in my case, but I had a feeling that in that madrigal rehearsal there was a chance to show the Dents that living in the house mightn't be the way to bliss. I believe they bought on impulse—lovely house, lovely weather, lovely view and the welcome feeling of being in the public eye. Then they realised that they'd underestimated their Vistamar neighbour. And speaking of Boris, do you believe for one moment that she would have let them live in peace? Have you ever known her, in all these years, fail to get what she went after?'

'No. All the same—'

'It would have been open warfare, with Rocksea on the side of Boris. I don't have to remind you that she wouldn't stop at anything, once—'

'—once she'd got her teeth in. Or Curzon's. That's correct; she might start off using fair means, but she thinks foul are more fun.'

They were driving back to the cottage after completing the details of the sale. Dinner was eaten in a mood of celebration; of them all, only Jeanne seemed to lack something of the joy and relief exhibited by the others.

When dinner was over, Roberta suggested going over to Cristall's for coffee. Jeanne pleaded fatigue, and Oliver said that he would stay behind to keep her company.

'You're tired,' he told her, when the others had gone. 'It wasn't just an excuse.'

'No, it wasn't. I'd like to have an early night.'

'Then come and sit on the sofa with me and I'll tell you a bedtime story.'

'No. Save it for the twins.'

She had turned away. He took her arm, not

267

a gentle hold, and made her face him.

'What's the matter with you?' he demanded.

'Nothing.'

'Yes, there is. Something's happened to you. Have you changed your mind about staying here?'

'I . . . I think so. Yes.'

'Why?'

'I thought it over. I only came here to . . . to stay for a little while before going on to France. It's been wonderful, and I'm grateful, but it's time I thought about the future.'

'I offered you a future. It didn't appear to me that you turned it down. In fact, you accepted it. You were perfectly prepared to consider staying permanently in this country. You understood what I said, and you understood what I didn't say. So why this talk of going away?'

'I've told you. I—'

His hold tightened.

'I know what's happened,' he said. 'You've been talking to Elva.'

He released her, but when she went towards the door, he stepped in front of her.

'Not talking to Elva,' he amended. 'Listening to her.' He seized a chair, dragged it forward and made her sit down. 'Now you're going to listen to me.'

'Look, please Oliver, I—'

'I didn't say talk. I said listen. In case you didn't take in what I was trying to tell you

268

about staying in this cottage, I'll repeat it. I shouldn't have to repeat it, because I think you know exactly what I meant. I wanted you to stay here because . . . well, why does a man ask a woman to stay in his house, live in his house, take over his house, if he doesn't feel very strongly about keeping her with him? I could have said to you: "Look, I know it sounds a bit swift, but I love you." I could have said: "I may be reading too much into this situation, but I feel you might be induced to admit that you love me." I didn't say it because I didn't think you were ready for it. I didn't say it because I didn't think you'd shaken yourself clear of Paul. Not emotionally; I wasn't worried about that. But I thought that you were still feeling the after-effects of a marriage that had gone wrong, and I decided to play safe, and go slow. So I asked you to stay, and you said you would, and now you say you won't and there's only one thing that can have made you change your mind so fast, and that is that you and Elva talked, and in the course of the conversation she remarked that Roberta wouldn't marry Austin because she was in love with me. Right?'

'I just told you—'

'Did she, or didn't she?'

'She—'

'Yes or no?'

'Yes.'

'Well, as far as it goes, it's true. Roberta has

been in love with me since she was sixteen. In between visits to Parson's House to tell me so, she told David and my mother, and she told her own father and mother whenever she chanced to see them, and she told all the men she took up for a time and dropped when she got tired of them. Her heart, she explained at some length, was mine; always mine; forever mine. The situation didn't hurt anyone, least of all Roberta. The only reason for its continuance was the fact that Roberta couldn't have me. As you've obviously no gift for sizing people up, you won't have noticed that women like Roberta get tired of anything that comes easily. She has gone through craze after craze, year after year, and I'm the only craze she didn't get tired of because I made it clear to her that she couldn't have me. She didn't give up writing about that crab because she wanted to paint. She was tired of him. She was tired of mosaics. She was tired of book-binding. She was tired of painting portraits. Do you think Austin would have come here, stayed here, remained one of us, if he'd imagined I'd ever take Roberta seriously? Like you, he would have packed up and run. But he and I had this out years ago. And so did Roberta and I. While I'm single, available, she'll keep up the fiction of being in love. Once I'm married, she'll go on as she's done for years, from one man to the next, until she wakes up one morning and glances at a calendar. And then she'll marry

Austin. And now that you've listened to the whole story, instead of a misleading line or two of it, will you for God's sake open your eyes and see how near you were to wrecking our chances of being happy?' He drew her to her feet and put his arms round her. 'You've frightened me,' he said. 'Every time something like this comes up in the future, are you going to run out on me, instead of stopping to check your facts?'

She shook her head. Tears were streaming down her cheeks. She fumbled for her handkerchief, found it, and he took it from her and wiped the tears away.

'This time, we'll lay it on the line,' he said. 'I love you, Madame Brisson. Do you love me?'

'Yes. I do.'

'Will you marry me?'

'Yes, I will.'

'We signed a compact once before,' he reminded her. 'This time it's going to be sealed and delivered to the press.' He picked her up and carried her to the sofa. 'And now for that bedtime story,' he said.

*   *   *

Roberta's congratulations on the following day were as warm as those of the others, but somewhat more outspoken.

'If I can't have him,' she said, 'there's nobody I'd give him to with more pleasure than to you. I told you, didn't I, the very first thing when you came here, that you needed a nest?'

'And there's one on offer,' Austin said. 'I've just become the owner of a haunted property. I had an idea of marrying and settling down in it, but marrying takes two, and the woman I have in mind likes time to consider. So I now offer it to you two. You'd be crazy not to live in it. You'd pay me rent and we could work out a way in which you could buy the house from me over a period of, say, a hundred years. Then I'll buy this cottage from Oliver and move in and wait for Roberta to join me. Any flaws in that?'

'Yes.' It was Jeanne who answered. 'It's more kind of you than I can say, but . . . No.'

'Reasons?' Austin asked.

'Only one reason. I want to live here.'

'In this cottage?'

'Yes. Perhaps before I came to live here, it might have been different. I know that Parson's House . . . we all have this special feeling for it. But if Oliver doesn't mind—'

'Oliver's in entire agreement,' Oliver said. 'I would have accepted Austin's offer if you'd wanted me to, but I like it better this way. I've looked on this cottage as mine ever since my mother married David and moved out of it. Whatever I feel about Parson's House, I've never felt this sense of ownership. So Austin can move in next door and put thick mattresses at the bottom of the stairs in case he ever does

272

anything to annoy the ghost.'

Austin's eyes went to Roberta.

'No,' she said. 'Keep a room for me. But I'm going to be in Turkey for the next few months. I'm going to a place called Kutahya, where there are about forty pottery factories. I'm going to study their old designs for tiles and their methods of putting the designs on to the tiles. But if you want any help with moving in before I go, just ask me.'

There was no need to ask her, or to ask anyone. Lady Cressing took charge. Finding Mr Quinter unwilling to finish the work of redecorating Parson's House, she called for volunteer workers from the town, and got them. Mrs Clermont refused to set foot in the house, and Lady Cressing did not waste any time in attempting to make her change her mind; she made other plans and communicated them triumphantly to Austin.

'It was no use trying to engage servants, only to have them imagining ghostly presences in the house,' she explained. 'The thing to do was to fish in other waters. You need a cook—a good cook—a houseman and a gardener. There's not enough work for a full-time gardener, so what I've arranged is that Suni's grandfather will give you four evenings a week. I've talked to him; he's only too delighted. Now for the cook: Suni's wife's uncle is a splendid cook; he worked in a restaurant before they all became refugees. He's free, and

273

he's coming and he will live next door and you must pay for his board and lodging. That was Grandfather's idea, and I must say it was a good one. His son—the wife's uncle's son—is to be your houseman, but he will live at Parson's House.'

'I'm very grateful,' Austin said with feeling.

'So you should be. I've worked very hard. Wages: that you must arrange yourself, but you must be very generous, because they need the money, and if it gets about and there's any jealousy or absurd talk about overpaying, I shall explain that you are bound to overpay in order to get people to work in a house with so sinister a reputation. Now tell me: what is this nonsense about Roberta and Turkey?'

'Well, she's going there for a time. She—'

'Send her to see me,' commanded Lady Cressing. 'Not at Vistamar. I'm going up to Parson's House with Oliver; you might just ask Roberta if she'd spare a little time to advise me about new curtains. Tell her I need her artist's eye.'

Roberta took her artist's eye, to find that it was not needed. All she was required to do was help Lady Cressing and Oliver to remove the dust covers from the furniture.

'I can't tell you,' Lady Cressing said, 'how I feel about being in this house again. I am so thankful, so very thankful! I feel as if I've wakened after a bad dream. Now, Roberta, before you go back to the cottage, I'd like to talk frankly to you. No, don't go, Oliver; you're as much concerned in this matter as I am. I'm going to talk about Austin.'

Oliver sat down.

'We all know,' Lady Cressing began, 'that for years, Roberta has refused to marry Austin. I'm not going to say that I'm sorry about this; that would be to understate. All I'll say is that I'm sorry a girl of your intelligence, Roberta, can't recognise what a splendid husband he would make. But your business is your business and I have no intention of interfering. My sole concern, as I said, is with Austin. He cannot be expected to be happy all alone in this house. He will of course have Oliver and the twins and Jeanne next door, but he will need, and he will certainly look for a companion for himself. He is young, he is extremely rich. We cannot claim good looks for him, but he has something better than looks: a pleasant personality. Add to all this the fact that he owns a beautiful house, and in no time at all we shall see him becoming the prey of designing women. Whatever the merits or demerits of marriage, it was, is and always will be the most effective mantrap known to women, and Austin will be no match for schemers. The first thing will be to save him from installing a mistress in his home.'

'He won't do that,' Roberta said.

'Oh? What makes you state that so confidently?'

'Well . . . he's not the type.'

'In this matter, there are no types. My plan is not only to keep out a mistress, but also to find him a wife. I have some charming unmarried grand-nieces; I saw three of them when I was in London recently, and I was pleased to see that they hadn't turned out at all like their parents. The first that comes to my mind is Parthenope, named after me, my eldest brother's child. She was rather plain when she was small, but she has improved and she is an excellent little housekeeper and would fit in very well here. If not her, there's Eulalia, her cousin, and Eulalia's sisters Millicent and Margaret. All well-brought-up, all presentable, and all far more interested in finding a husband than in painting Turkish tiles. Not that I have any fears for your future, Roberta, my dear. You are still young, and there is no doubt that when your sense of values sharpens a little, you will find a good husband, and I hpoe you will bring him to see us sometimes, though one can't of course hope that he will ever be one of us in the sense that Austin is. But I want to assure you both, as you have his welfare at heart, that I will find a wife for dear, dear, Austin.'

'Austin can look after himself, can't he?' Roberta asked.

'I think not. With a happy married couple living next door to him, he will long for a wife. Underneath that light-hearted manner of his,

276

there is a great deal of passion.'

Oliver, listening, marvelled. In ten minutes, he thought, she would have them believing it. In ten more, she would convince Austin.

Lady Cressing rose.

'Now you mustn't keep me,' she said. 'I have plans, and I don't like grass to grow under my feet. You must come and say goodbye to me before you go, Roberta dear.'

Oliver, at the cottage, poured two drinks and handed one to Roberta.

'To Austin's future,' he said. 'Safe in Boris's keeping.'

Roberta put down her glass untouched.

'Did she mean all that bit about importing her nieces?' she asked.

'Grand-nieces. Yes, she meant it. But as you said, he can look after himself.'

'Not against Boris, he can't. He won't stand a chance.'

'Wouldn't you rather see him safe with one of her selections rather than lusting after the local loose ladies?'

'He doesn't lust after. You know that as well as I do.'

'A vacuum has to be filled. I'll try to see she doesn't bulldoze him into anything, but I shan't be here all the time. I think you can safely leave it to Boris.'

'And let her install an outsider at Parson's House? Is that what you'd like to see? Some woman we've never heard of, some woman who might turn out to be a prize-winning bitch, who'd take over Parson's House, who might even object to Elva having a permanent room there? Just think what it would be like!'

'I'll try not to think. If you try to think, you might see that his getting landed with a wife you might not approve of is a lot better than letting him hang about for another ten years or so waiting for someone he wants to make up her mind. Underneath that light-hearted manner of his, there's a great deal too much patience. He's hung on because he's a humble fellow and he didn't think his merits were outstanding enough to strike you all at once. He's hung on because he didn't think a humdrum chap like himself should stop you from executing all those brilliant artistic feats like binding a couple of books or putting together a couple of mosaics or drawing a few squiggles on tiles. So you just go on being brilliant and let Boris do something about making him happy. You don't want him, so let him go to somebody else. If his wife shuts you out of Parson's House, you can drop in next door and Jeanne and I will put you up. And if you want another drink, you'll have to get it yourself, because I'm going down to have a swim.'

Jeanne, drying herself after racing him to the rock, suspended the operation in order to subject him to a long study.

'What's the matter with you?' she asked.

'Nothing. Why?'

'You keep smiling all to yourself. What are you thinking about?'

'Roberta. Want to make a bet?'

'No.'

'Then I won't tell you what I'm thinking about.'

'All right, then.'

'If I'm right, you pay me a pound. If I'm wrong, I pay you. Agreed?'

'Yes. But I don't know what I'm betting about.'

'Roberta's trip to Turkey.'

'Has she changed her mind?'

'She will.'

'You're sure?'

'If I were certain, I wouldn't bet, would I?'

'You might. When we were young . . .'

She stopped; he had taken her into his arms and was murmuring into her wet strands of hair.

'Oh Jeanne, Jeanne, Jeanne, how happy we're all going to be . . .'

She paid up the following morning. All five were present at the cottage, but Jeanne, handing over the note to Oliver, said nothing, and he pocketed it without comment.

They then gave their minds to the wedding arrangements. Jeanne and Oliver's was to be a quiet affair, and would take place a week before Roberta and Austin's—but Roberta gave notice that she was going to take full advantage of this opportunity of being the centre of attention, and wanted all the trimmings, with the twins in attendance.

'They'll enjoy that,' Jeanne said. 'They can wear those pretty dresses I bought in . . .'

'Most certainly not,' Roberta said in Boris's own tone. 'I've got my own ideas on what they're going to wear at my wedding. Do you think I ought to invite my parents? They could talk to Elva's father and Mrs Selby.'

'We seem to be in the way,' Oliver told Austin. 'How about going over to Cristall's and leaving them to it?'

Austin, in a state too bemused to argue, followed him to the door. Then he paused.

'I was just thinking,' he said.

'Save it,' Oliver advised. 'They're not interested.'

'Yes, we are,' Elva said. 'What is it?'

'It was about that tune, la la la, ta ta, la. Can't sing it, but the words are something about Now thank we all our God. Is it a madrigal, or a carol?'

'It's neither. It's a hymn,' Roberta said. 'But it isn't a wedding hymn, if that's what you're thinking of.'

'No. I'm thinking of adapting it for madrigal singers,' Austin said. 'With a solo part for myself.'

'Head notes?' Elva asked him.

'No. Straight from the heart,' he said.